1758Katja/41,381 words
11/27/2018

Katja

Sequel to the Irwin Glass trilogy
By
Harley L. Sachs

Harley Sachs

Cover photo of Nisha, used by permission.

Paperback ISBN 9-781-939381-50-7
Ebook ISBN 9-781-939381-50-4

Books by Harley L. Sachs:

Novels

Queer Company
Never Trust a Talking Horse
The Gold Chromosome
Murder by Mail (Scratch—out!)!
Ben Zakkai's Coffin
The Search for Jesse Bram
The Mystery Club Solves a Murder
The Mystery Club and the Dead Doctor
The Mystery Club and the Hidden Witness
The Mystery Club and the Serial Widow
Deliver me From Evil
White Slave
Conspiracy!
Murder in the Keweenaw
The Lollipop Murder
Betrayal
Retribution
Burnt Out
Katja
Sam in Love
StopRape.com
The Accidental Courier
Dead Men Don't Bleed
Metadata Man: The Seventh Paradigm
The Metadata Curse
Metadata Man: Internet Cope

Collections of short fiction

Ahoy! Quarterdeck! (Irma Quarterdeck Reports)
Anna-Lena's Troll and other stories
Threads of the Covenant: The Jews of Red Jacket
Yooper Tales and Other Funny Stuff
Misplaced Persons

Non-Fiction

Freelance Non-Fiction Articles
The Misadventures of Cpl. Sachs

Harley L. Sachs

The 1957 Sachs Arctic Expedition
From Tent to Castle: Memoir of a Year-Long Honeymoon
IS
Chilly-Chilly BANG! How We Freelanced Through Europe's Coldest Winter in a
 VW with a Kid
Essays and Columns: 1992-2011
The Writing Life
Cartoons
Hunting the Mail Buoy and other hazards to navigation

Author's Note

"Katja" is the sequel to the Irwin Glass trilogy, "Betrayal," "Retribution," and "Burnt Out." From the time Katja turned up outside the office of Irwin Glass, instructor at Michigan Institute of Technology, claiming she is his daughter, she was an enigma. She is beautiful, sexy, and alluring but she is also a trained cold-blooded killer who carries a Glock 9 millimeter pistol. As his alleged daughter, she becomes a dangerous member of Irwin's household. The FBI claim she is a sleeper agent, suggesting there is a trigger to activate her for her ultimate mission, but what is it? When Irwin, Ivy and baby Isaac join Katja in Portland, Oregon, we find out, but how do you cure a trained assassin of homicidal tendencies?

Prologue

Portland, Oregon

Dear Irwin,

I hope you not mind if I call you Irwin.. I know you are my biological father, but even living with you as your Russian daughter I did not get used to calling you papa or dad. Vladimir is my real Russian father even though he said I was my mother's child and not his.

Some people say no child is illegitimate. It is not the child's fault. But, Like Bible says, the sins of the father descend to the children for many generations.

Of course, I am also the sin of my mother. Her having me was her rebellion, her revenge for Vladimir's forcing her to pose for those honey pot photos. So here we are, you with a Russian daughter and Vladimir my mother's ruthless husband. The ways of an old KGB do not change easily. That is a story I live with even though it is hard to explain to people. There is betrayal and possible reconciliation, but not love. I do not think KGB colonels are capable of love.

At least you accept me. It is important to be accepted. I think you even love me as your surprise daughter. I hope so. When I was growing up in Moscow I felt rejected. If my mother hadn't told me about you when she was dying of cancer I would never have known. I think the only reason Vladimir says he accepted me is because he wanted to use me. He uses people, saw me as an asset. a cover for hiding stolen money. That's his way.

I know you do not like to telephone because you think you are on an FBI watch list. You do not use emails, either. Vladimir says a hand written letter sent by snail mail is the last secure way to communicate in this police state. He taught me that much. He should know, being ex-KGB from the old days.

Snail mail may be old fashioned, but here we are.

I'm sorry I left Michigan so suddenly. I did not wish to stay after the incident at Adat Israel synagogue. I did not wish to wait for an autopsy of that Palestinian, just in case they found my bullet in his thigh..

I transferred my credits at Michigan Institute of Technology to Portland State in Portland, Oregon. Now I use the name Katie Glass. I hope you not mind.

Portland was Vladimir's suggestion.. When he was given political asylum he wanted to get far away from Washington.. He still has the money he stole from Russian Mafia. He is doing all right, as long as they don't kill him.

He bought a private security company. Instead of KGB now he hires security guards for shopping malls. and strip clubs. It is not real police, but I think an easy move for him.

When I left Michigan you and Ivy were expecting a baby, a boy, so by now I now must have a half brother. Please tell me about it.

I miss you and Ivy. You became my American family. Without you I would be very lonely. Only family can share our secrets. Please write.

Your Russian daughter,

Katja.

Dear Katja (or Katie, whichever you like),

How wonderful to hear from you! A lot has happened and I will try to bring you up to date. !Yes, Ivy had our little boy Isaac Meelamud Harftshorne-Glass. Seven pounds three ounces, as if a baby were an angler's prize fish. What's important is that he is normal-- ten fingers and ten toes. In deference to my family roots which turned up in my DNA, we had him circumcised. I enclose his baby pictures.

So much for my good news. The bad news is I did not get tenure. My job at Michigan Institute of Technology was to teach bonehead English to foreign students and beginning Russian, but nobody signed up for the Russian classes.

The Moslem students quickly realized I was an FBI informant on their activities and would not have me as their faculty advisor. He two students who were interdicted put a stain on my career. I was shunned by the Moslem students and by the Marxist faculty in the department. They simply wanted me out. Denying me tenure was their easy choice. So now I must either find another job or reconcile to being a house husband baby sitter while Ivy earns our living.

Ivy is not happy with our situation. She is also tired of the long winters here in the UP and would rather be near her parents in Ocala, Florida. There is a university there where she can teach German.

Honestly, I think Ivy just wanted to be married and have a child. I was convenient, but now that she has our legitimate son Isaac she is satisfied. I feel like the honey bee drone: once the queen is impregnated, the drone is useless and kicked out of the hive. From Ivy's point of view as queen bee, I have done my bit, so maybe I should get out.

Is this how we use one another? It's not fair.For now it's not a divorce, just an estrangement, I suppose until she makes up her mind about a divorce or finds someone else.

It sounds like Vladimer Putinsky and I have something in common, children-wise. To have a kid and not have a kid. Apology to Shakespeare.

Maybe you have a suggestion?

Maybe you and I could somehow get together, father and so-called daughter. Could do worse.Like you say, everyone needs family.

Any jobs for Russian teachers in Portland?

Your American dad,

Irwin

Dear Irwin,

Thank you for the pictures of my little brother Isaac. I see that Ivy is nursing. How do you manage that if you are both still teaching? Do you pass the baby back and forth between classes like a football?

Will you follow Ivy to Florida? Does she plan to stay with her parents? You told me once they live in a trailer court. Mrs. Hartshorne does some kind of sewing and uses the spare bedroom for her hobby. Does that mean Ivy and the baby have to stay in the lanai? Would Mrs. Hartshorne be happy with a baby in the house?

I think she is a woman not very patient or willing to share her space.

Some grannies will cuddle a baby only til it needs its diaper changed.

It is like summer here in Oregon, but March in the Copper Country is the worst time of winter. I can't imagine taking a baby out of doors in that.

I think you should get on Internet and research Portland schools. There are half a dozen colleges here. PSU is the largest university, but there is university of Portland and several two year colleges.

March is bad time of year in Copper Country. The winter is long and never seems to end. Add to that your losing your job and possible divorce from Ivy and your son is not good. Looking for a new place to work may lift you out of your spring time depression. Everyone needs something to look forward to.

I will ask Vladimere if he has job for you. I do not see you as security guard at a strip club. There are five thousand Russians in Portland and Ukrainians. There are Russian grocery stores and restaurants. You could feel at home even though you were never in Russia more than a few months..

Thanks to Vladimere's stolen Mafia money, as long as it lasts, I can afford a nice apartment near the campus on the south Park Blocks. The Avalon Arms is a secure building, but there has been some crime here. For safety I have a concealed carry permit for my Glock.

Maybe I should not tell you that. I know how you feel about guns.

Let me know what progress you make and what you decide.

Your adopted Russian daughter,

Katja

Dear Katja,

(I cannot get used to Katie. To me you will always be Katja)

So many questions! Yes, the winter has been long, but we survived the usual St. Patrick's Day blizzard. On Father's Day last year we had an unusual cloudburst and a flood that took out many roads and bridges. The winter that followed has been severe. Ivy and I can hardly wait to get out of here.

I said that Ivy wanted to get married so she could have a legitimate baby. She is not one of those who opt for childbirth without a husband. I do not think it is easy to be a single parent, if that is her choice

There is more to our failing relationship than that. She blames me for what happened to the two Moslem students. It was not my fault.

It was a misunderstanding. Whatever the reason, the result was a disaster. Now Ivy sees me as some kind of evil person. I was only being helpful to the local FBI. I have to admit I was used. Once you have lost someone's trust, you are finished.

In Moscow Vladimere wanted to force me to supply the KGB with information. Then in Michigan the FBI wanted me to inform on my foreign students. How ironic! We live in parallel worlds. I want no part of either.

So you are still carrying that Glock! I guess for you it's a security blanket. Is it legal at Portland State for students to pack heat, as they say? Tell me about the college.

Have you changed majors?

I do not think I would want to work for Vladimere. He is too controlling, too sinister. It would be ironic if I refused to work for him when he was KGB in Moscow and ended up being his lackey guarding a strip club in Portland. I'd rather be a greeter at Wal-Mart.

I can see that nowadays it is almost impossible to get a tenure track position at any college even if I had a Ph.D. I maight be doomed to be one of those itinerant teachers, forever an adjunct, never full time anywhere. One is always on square one. Cancel a class and you can't make the rent. Why would anyone invest In a PhD for that? That's what has happened to higher education.

At least, paid for with stolen Russian Mafia money, you do not need to go into debt with student loans.

Your caring American dad,

Irwin.

Dear Irwin,

I was worried when I did not hear from you. Your post card from Ocala, Florida said only that you arrived, no return address, so I hope this will be forwarded to wherever you are. Please write. If you come to Portland you can stay with me.

Katja

Dear Katja,

No need for you to put up with my awful handwriting. I bought an old used portable Royal typewriter at the Ocala Goodwill store. It is older than any computer on the market, but typewriters do not go obsolete as long as you can find ribbons.

Yes, we are in Florida. It was a harrowing trip. Ivy and I loaded our stuff in the back of my old pickup truck, covered it with a tarp, and with Isaac in a carrier between us on the front seat headed south.

We never had much furniture, had only rented the old house near the campus in Houghton, so what we did have wasn't worth paying a moving company. We felt like Oakies fleeing the dust bowl in The Grapes of Wrath. Being

Russian, you probably never saw that movie. Fortunately, Ivy was nursing so we didn't have the complications of baby formula and bottles to sterilize. Diapers were disposable.

It took almost a week to get to Florida. I had to replace the Toyota's old snow tires and a fuel pump, which delayed us. Then when we got to the Hartshornes,'Ivy's father was sick. We are not exactly welcome.

Many children, saddled with student debt, end up living in their parent's garage, even for years. That's not the way things are supposed to go. You are expected to get good jobs, buy a house, and live the middle class life. What happened to America? It's like we failed.

Ivy did get a contract for a part time job at University of Florida but does not start until September, so we are living on our savings until she starts collecting a pay check.

I feel like an unwelcome relative, which I guess I am even if I'm married to the Hartshornes' daughter. They say relatives and fish stink after three days. There is only one bathroom. The lanai is nothing but a screened in porch. We have out lasted that welcome.

This trailer park is intended for senior citizens. Visiting grandchildren like Isaac are tolerated, even though he is a baby, not running around the neighborhood and making mischief. For fussy neighbors a resident Peacock screeching is bad enough, but a baby crying?

I have applied for a teaching job in Portland at PCC, Portland Community College and another school in Gresham, wherever that is. No interview trip. Too expensive for the schools to bring me across the country. Apparently Portland is a magnet for educated people who all want jobs.

Ivy says she will write to you, and tell her side of our story.

Your doting American dad,

Irwin

Dear Katya,

Irwin gave me your address in Portland. When you took off we were worried about you but you had done it before.

We are now living in Ocala with my parents, but it's not a good situation. I think they could put up with me if I were alone. When my new job starts my mother can baby sit while I am teaching. Some grandmas dote on babies. My mother doesn't have the patience. Diapers? She said she did that before and had enough of it. She was happy enough to show Isaac off to the neighbors, but then handed him back so she could go off for coffee with the "girls."

Irwin, I'm afraid, is depressed.

Irwin is still in shock and feels guilty about what happened to those two Arab students. He should be. I'm sorry to say that though I still love Irwin, after what happened I cannot live with him. Those boys were not terrorists. Irwin says it was all a misunderstanding.

I'm very conflicted. We should find a counselor for advice.

Irwin does not think Russian is a good opportunity for teaching in Florida. He says you suggest he find a job in Portland where there are lots of Russians. That is about as far away as you can get from Ocala without going to Alaska or Hawaii. If he moves west, how will he ever see our son Isaac? A boy needs a father figure.

I guess it is not uncommon for husbands to abandon their families, but Irwin is not like that. He's a person of loyalty, so he is conflicted, too.

It would be easier if you weren't so far away. Does Putinsky have that much hold on you? When he was being interrogated at the farm outside Washington I could see he's a tough customer. I could never have a man like that as a friend, but he is your Russian father and your meal ticket.

I wouldn't be surprised if the Russian Mafia killed him. They tried before. You got us out of that scrape in Houghton but you were lucky. We were all lucky.

Maybe you should change your name. You are more of a Glass than a Putinsky. We could adopt you, officially. Or Irwin could. If we get a divorce I will keep my maiden name. See how confusing it all is?

Now Isaac is crying. Time to feed him. Irwin says he envies the bonding nursing mothers have with their babies. He doesn't realize how it is when the baby gets teeth. Isaac has two baby teeth.

Love,

Ivy

Dear Irwin,

Of course I saw "The Grapes of Wrath." It was shown in Russia to prove Capitalism was failure. We also read Mark Twain's books because of the slavery issue.

Vladimir has bought himself an apartment in the Mirabella. It is a luxury retirement building near the river. He likes it because it is high security. It is also on the streetcar line and close to OHSU hospital.

It is hot this summer in Portland and very dry. Forest fires make the air smoky, but soon it will be raining again, all winter. You will need a good raincoat. You can donate those Yooper boots to Goodwill. It almost never snows here.

When are you coming? The sooner the better if you want to find a teaching job. Or you could work for Vladimere, put on a uniform and badge and be a rent a cop at a shopping mall.

Security guards are just for show. You cannot have a weapon, just a radio to call the real police. The security guard uniform and badge do no more than intimidate. Recently a team of four grab and run thieves rushed through an Apple store, stole a fortune and were gone in twenty seconds before security guards could react. So much for that job!.

Vladimere told me if the guards locked the doors to keep the thieves from running away it would be kidnapping. If they had arms and drew them it would be brandishing, another offense. The criminals have the advantage. I'm afraid if I'd been a guard I'd have shot them. I could have got all four in four seconds, head shots, but then I would be murderer. Stealing computers is not a capital offense. Shooting unarmed thief is. I think better you should teach.

So when are you coming? I have only one bedroom, but you can couch surf like a homeless student until you are settled.

I have a parking place in the garage for your pickup truck.

Come soon. I miss you, my American papa.

Katja

CHAPTER ONE

The Sunset Village senior center park avoided the name "trailer" though the residents all lived in single or double wide manufactured homes that had to be anchored to resist being blown away if the next hurricane made it inland to Ocala, Florida. Residents mainly owned their homes, but paid rent on the spaces where they were parked. Rent for the spaces included hookups for electricity, water, sewage, and weekly garbage pickup. Thanks to current technology, a senior could order groceries on line from   Win-Dixie   which were delivered by golf cart.

Bill Hartshorne could do the shopping from his Lay-Z-Boy recliner which was his virtual home since his heart attack. Mostly he watched 24 hour CNN cable news and sports. The only time he left the house was his daily breakfast walk down to the Kracker Koffee shop where he lingered with the regulars until the waitress gave them the fish eye and asked if they wanted to order lunch.

The Harzhornes did own a car, a faded maroon Buick, parked, moldering in the sun on the street in front of their place. Once a week Mrs. Hartzhorne would start the engine so the battery would not go totally flat. When she did drive to the yarn store the car left an oily stain that would have warned her of an impending engine failure if she cared to look or understood what it meant.

They could have sold the car, for the preferred form of local senior transportation was an electric golf cart which could be driven on the sidewalks but was a menace in the street traffic. A golf cart had no brake lights or turn signals. They also did not require a driver's license, a plus for octogenarians with cataracts or macular degeneration.

The Hartzhornes didn't have a garage. What could have passed for a car port or even a garage was the lanai, a porch screened in against the Florida bugs. If there was a breeze in the stifling Florida summer, that was where they could catch it. For privacy and against rain and wind blinds could be lowered. This is where Ivy and Irwin landed with baby Isaac in their exile from the snows of the Upper Peninsula of Michigan.

Irwin hated it. He hated being essentially fired from his job at Michigan Institute of Technology. He hated being a patsy for Mr. Wilkins, the Marquette FBI agent. He hated being jobless. He hated the prospect of becoming an itinerant perpetual adjunct instructor with no hope of the tenure that provided job stability. It had taken a long time to recover from the humiliation of losing his foreign service job in Moscow so many years ago. He'd had to start over, and here he was again only this time with a wife and a baby.

Looking out the window at the quiet street he saw a red roadster, the kind of car one sometimes sees with a geezer at the wheel and a trophy blonde beside him. Only in this case there were two men, young and healthy, Hawaiian shirts, baseball caps and dark sunglasses. If they had been wearing white shirts and the prerequisite neckties Irwin might have taken them for Latter Day Saints missionaries. These men, however, had a different mission.

They both extricated their long legs from the front seat of the roadster and confidently approached the Hartshorne residence. Their body language showed they were not tourists uncertain of where they were going. Instead, they walked like cops, a sense of authority easily spotted when men like that walk, for instance, into a bar. But these two wore golfers' shorts. Their shirts were not tucked in, but hung out so they could conceal a gun carried in the small of their backs. Irwin was pretty sure who they were before they got to the Hartshorne's door.

Before they could knock, Irwin met them.

One held up an ID card and asked, "Irwin Glass?"

"Nice shirt," Irwin said. The shirts were almost identical, one blue and one orange, and might have been bought off the same rack. "I thought you guys drove black, armored SUVs."

"That's the Secret Service in Washington," the second man, orange shirt, said. "This is Florida."

"Come in," Irwin offered, not that he could have kept them out.

"Who is it?" Mr. Hartshorne called from his recliner.

"I think they're selling insurance," Irwin quipped.

"Tell them we don't need any."

Blue shirt, the older first agent, smiled, understanding that Irwin respected the need for confidentiality, whatever their business was.

"There's the Kracker Koffee shop a block away," Irwin suggested then remembered the crowd of gossipy old men who hung out there. "But they have a CCT camera. Maybe we could talk in the park."

The two men agreed.

Irwin called, "I'm going to show them around the complex." Then, to fill in the lie, added, "We have a recreation center with a screened in swimming pool, shuffle board court, and hot tub. Also a tennis court, if you brought your rackets."

When he joined the two agents on the street Irwin paused before squeezing into the tiny back seat. He noticed a set of manacles on the floor. "Those for me?"

Blue shirt, the driver, looked over his shoulder. "Maybe another time."

"This about those two students that got interdicted?"

The partner explained. "No. It's about your alleged daughter Katja."

"Alleged?" That brought back the whole business of the "is she or isn't she?" confusion that ended, he thought, with the DNA confirmation. It was called prima fascia evidence meaning she was definitely his biological daughter and, being the daughter of a US citizen, entitled to a US passport. Which she got. Did she still have her Russian passport? Did she have dual citizenship? Too many mysteries. He didn't want to go there.

The agents apparently knew Ocala well. "We can take a walk in Tuscawilla Park."

Irwin had never been there. He and Ivy had not done any sightseeing.

It was still early in the day, before the Florida heat set in. They walked along the lake with its fountain, one agent on each side like Irwin was being escorted from a court. At least he wasn't handcuffed and didn't need to pull a jacket over his face if he wore one. "So what about Katja? Did Agent Wilkins of Marquette brief you?"

The two men were silent. Irwin did not know their names. Instead of introducing themselves they just flashed their IDs. Irwin tried another line of questions. "How did you find me?"

"Your wife left a forwarding address with the college.> Simple enough.

The other added, "And we followed your Visa card purchases--motel registrations , gas in Green Bay, a tire purchase in Indiana, fuel pump repair in Kentucky. You had a difficult trip."

Irwin couldn't resist the sarcasm. "Sure you didn't put a tracker in my pickup truck? I don't even carry a cell phone."

Orange shirt laughed. "Your wife has a cell phone." He turned to fix a warning look at Irwin. "We always know where you are."

Irwin suppressed a shudder. "Nice to know I have protection."

Blue shirt: "You're not that hard to follow. Katja is."

"So what's your interest in Katja? Did they do an autopsy on the Palestinian kid that got squashed by a logging truck?"

The agents looked at each other, deciding whether or not they should follow up on that line of questions. The second got to their main point. "We need to know more about your Russian daughter."

"She's changed her name to Katie Glass. I suppose you already know that."

Their body language said they didn't. Irwin immediately regretted letting them know her alias.

The agents stopped and, after cautiously looking around, settled on a bench facing the lake.

Irwin explained, "Putinsky's set himself up with a private security company. Katja said Vladimir could get me a job guarding a strip club. Apparently Portland has two hundred nude dancing so-called gentlemen's clubs. I don't see myself being a bouncer facing down a bunch of horny drunks."

The first agent gave Irwin an assessing look. "You're not the type."

Which type? Horny drunk or beefy bouncer? Irwin didn't know whether that was an insult or not. "Right. So what's your problem? Why did you track me down?"

They paused. Finally, blue shirt, who seemed to be in charge said, "We think your Katja or Katie is a sleeper agent. We think she was recruited in Moscow and trained to use the legend, the cover story, that she's your daughter."

"You think?"

Orange shirt ignored his partner's caution and said, "We got a tip. A defector included her during his debriefing, didn't know the girl's name, but the conclusion was obvious."

Irwin protested. Katja had become part of his family. "But she is my daughter. The DNA…"

"Faked."

Irwin took a deep breath. He had feared it was all a ruse, but Katja was in Portland and he was in Florida. So what? "Ivy and I may get a divorce. Katja wants me to look for a job in Oregon."

Orange shirt: "You should go. We could use you."

Blue shirt shook his head. "I can just see you in a uniform with a badge ' Irwin Glass rent a cop.'" He laughed

Irwin felt insulted. "So what do you want me to do? Be an FBI informant on my own daughter?"

Put it that way, the two agents didn't answer.

It was bad enough that Wilkins had him informing on the Moslem students' Association. It was terrible that the result was two innocent--for all he knew-- students being interdicted. Shipped secretly out of the country by the CIA or whoever to be water boarded in some foreign place. Then, when one died, he, Irwin Glass, had the distressing task of helping the distraught parents pick up their son's belongings to return to their home country. His own guilt had nearly given him a nervous breakdown.

He took a deep breath and tried to control his anger and anguish. "You guys are in the wrong country. You should be with the Stasi secret police in East Germany."

"East Germany is reunified."

"So what? You expect Americans to report on their own children?"

"She's not your child."

"Bullshit. This whole business is crap. We don't report on our own families."

"Where's your loyalty to your country?"

Irwin shook his head. "My loyalty is to the constitution. That's the oath you guys took yourselves. There's nothing in the constitution about betraying your own family."

"Harboring a foreign agent is conspiracy. You can go to jail for that."

Irwin remembered the manacles on the floor of the back seat of the roadster. "I'm not harboring anybody. I'm just trying to live a normal life with my wife and our baby."

"Living in a lanai with no privacy is hardly normal."

Irwin shook his head. "That's not your problem. It's mine."

"We may have a solution. What if we set you up with a job in Portland?"

"I'm not going to be a security guard for naked pole dancers."

"No. A real job. The government has connections."

Irwin suddenly recalled the Rosenberg case. The couple had been ratted out by Greenglass. What was he? A relative or a friend? Greenglass got off. The Rosenbergs were executed. Would Katja go to the gas chamber? Or just deported in exchange for American spies imprisoned in Russia as bargaining chips? It was horrible.

All Irwin wanted was to get away from those two agents. How could he put them off? What would Ivy say to all this? "Make me an offer," he suggested. "Now if you don't mind, take me back to Sunset Village."

CHAPTER TWO

Ocala was too far north for coconut palms, but there were plenty of palmettos and other semi-tropical plants, a latitude in the transition zone between the deep south of Georgia and the tropics of the Keys.

Ivy had watched Irwin drive off with the two men in the red roadster. She waited by the picture window, her nursing blouse partly buttoned. She was holding Isaac against her shoulder, rubbing his back to get him to burp. "Who were those men?"

Irwin led her into the lanai and closed the sliding glass door. "FBI. They tracked us here."

She saw that he was furious. "What for? I thought you were done."

"So did I. They're interested in Katja. They claim she's a sleeper agent for Russia."

Isaac burped, spit up on the towel Ivy had on her shoulder. She wiped his mouth and put him down in his crib. "We were never sure about that."

"She's just a student."

Ivy laughed. "Irwin you are so naïve. What student carries a Glock and is a crack shot?"

He had to admit Katja must have had training. It was hard for him to connect the girl whose underwear had hung to dry in their shower in Michigan with some sort of secret agent. He stubbornly clung to his own fantasy. "But she's our daughter."

"Your daughter."

Irwin shrugged. "She's family."

"So what are you going to do?"

"They say they could fix me up with some sort of job in Portland."

"What? As a foreign student advisor to send some Saudis to their deaths?"

"Never."

"Then what?"

Irwin sighed. "I don't know. They might be our ticket out of Ocala."

"Your ticket."

He'd forgotten. He'd been in denial about her proposed separation. He'd hoped they would stay together. Now she'd reminded him. "I don't know what to do."

Ivy fixed a cold, analytical gaze on him. "Tell her. See how she reacts."

"Then what? Confess? Get her to tell her story, whatever that really is? She's an American citizen now. She can do as she pleases."

Irwin and Ivy had both gone to the Virginia Farm where Irwin assisted in the interrogation of Vladimir Putinsky. Putinsky was awarded political asylum and kept the fortune he'd stolen from the Russian Mafia.

Ivy's marriage to Irwin had been convenient because Ivy wanted a child. This would be her last chance because of that biological clock thing. Irwin was convenient and easy but not the great, consuming passion she might have hoped for. Katja's presence in their household as his beautiful, voluptuous Russian would-be daughter made Ivy jealous. "I saw the way you looked at her. If she's not your real daughter, why don't you move in with her as your mistress?"

She said this with bitterness, or was it jealousy?.

Irwin protested. "That's incest."

Ivy grinned and licked her lips with unaccustomed lasciviousness. "Not if she's not your real daughter, Irwin." Now she was teasing, goading him to admit lust for his daughter.

"Oh, my god, Ivy. are you pimping our daughter?"

Ivy's smile was not sincere. "Just testing you."

"Are you testing me to see which I would prefer? You or Katja? You're my wife, for Chris's sake."

"If you go out to be with her in Portland with me here in Ocala with Isaac, you will have made that choice."

"If I go to Oregon I want you to be with me."

"Seriously?"

"I'm a Midwesterner at heart. We take marriage vows to heart."

"That's all?"

Irwin sighed. "It might be different if we didn't have a kid. Now we have Isaac. There's a responsibility there."

He would never say so, but he had to admit Katja was a sexy young woman. Physically, he was tempted. Ivy was not as stacked, was on the skinny side. Katja resembled her mother, the voluptuous woman who exuded sex and had seduced him in Moscow. The images of their faces tended to blend. In Katja he saw the face of her mother, the woman in the red spaghetti strap evening dress that dropped to the floor in that hotel room and…

On the other hand, he knew Ivy. Katja was an unknown, mysterious quantity. One minute she could be cold, without remorse. The next she could be sentimental, as she was when he gave her that Teddy bear and pinned to it the Russian star from his souvenir winter hat. He could not forget how quickly she shot that home invader in Houghton. Pit bulls are friendly dogs, but can suddenly turn on their masters. Katja wasn't a dog, but she was more dangerous. He didn't know what might set her off and was afraid.

He tried to put the temptation of sexy Katja out of his mind. "I'll warn her."

"What will those two FBI agents think about that?"

Irwin was bitter. "Screw the FBI."

"It's your funeral."

CHAPTER THREE

Ivy's mother came to the door to the lanai. "What are you two arguing about?"

Irwin just shook his head without answering.

Ivy explained. "Irwin got a visit from the FBI."

"What does the FBI have to do with Irwin?"

Irwin explained. "There was an incident at my college in Michigan. Some Arab students got kidnapped by the CIA. One died."

Ivy added, "Irwin was faculty advisor for the Moslem students. The FBI thought they were terrorists."

"But they weren't," Irwin explained. "It was all a mistake."

Mrs. Hartshorne cautioned. "Don't tell your father about that."

It was good advice. Bill Hartshorne was something of an Islamophobe.

When she went back inside the house Irwin had calmed down. "You know how I am about cell phone calls. Your folks have a land line. Maybe we can call Katja."

"You going to tell her about the FBI? Confront her?"

"You know NSA monitors calls, and with the FBI watching me, I don't trust cell phones. Maybe you can ask her to call us back on your folk's land line, use a university telephone."

"Portland is three hours earlier than here."

"Wait a bit. When your dad goes out for his coffee and your Mom's in her sewing room, it might be OK."

They waited. Noon in Ocala was nine AM in Portland. Mr. Hartshorne had not come back from Kracker Koffee. Isaac was asleep so they went to the phone in the living room. It was on a table beside Mr. Hartshorne's recliner chair.

Irwin dialed Katja's cell phone number. No answer. They got voice mail, so Irwin asked that Katja call from a land line to the Hartshorne's home phone. It was confidential stuff.

There was no telling when she would call back.

Bill Hartshorne returned, made a pit stop to unload the Kracker Koffee and settled in his chair. The TV was turned on again, CNN, as usual, some panel chit-chatting about the president.

They waited.

For lunch Mr. Hartshorne took a sandwich and a beer to the table beside his chair and switched to a sports channel. The phone rang.

Mr. Hartshorne wasn't big on phone protocol. "Yeh? Who's this?" He called to the lanai. "Irwin, there's some girl on the line wants to talk to you."

Irwin said, "I'll take it in the kitchen extension." In the kitchen, the wall phone was appropriately the color of lemons or vanilla pudding. "Hello? Katja?"

She was puzzled. "I could not use university phone for long distance. I had to find a pay phone. There are not many of those left. Got to be quick, Irwin. I not have much change."

She could have used a credit card for the call, but, like Irwin, understood that there'd be a record on her account.

Irwin took a deep breath. "The FBI were here. They claim that you are a sleeper agent for the Russians. Just thought you should know."

She didn't respond right away, so Irwin continued. "They also say you are not my real daughter."

"But I am your daughter."

He could sense the stress in her voice. It would have been so much better to tell her face to face. "I know that. But I wanted you to know the situation before I make plans to move to Portland. The reason for this land line call is, you know, I'm spooked by NSA snooping on cell phone calls."

"Maybe we should speak Russian."

Irwin switched to Katja's mother tongue only long enough to say he'd write to her about it and goodbye.

When he returned to the living room Ivy's father was just hanging up the phone. "What the hell was that about? You have a Russian daughter?"

"It's a long story." Irwin sighed. "If Mrs. Hartshorne hears about it she'll blab to the whole knitting and yarn club. Everybody who sits around the pool and gossips. And you'll tell all those old guys hanging around Kracker Koffee."

"Everybody likes a good story, Irwin. So you have a Russian daughter?"

Irwin tried to brush it off. "Every bachelor's nightmare. I had a one night stand twenty years ago in Moscow. Lost my job over it. Could happen to anybody."

"Never happened to me," Ivy's father said, with a look of envy that suggested he had a new attitude toward his son-in-law.

Irwin put his finger to his nose like an old con artist. "Man to man stuff."

"Tell me about it." How could he tell and not tell? "I had no idea until Katja showed up outside my office and said I was her father."

Bill Hartshorne laughed. "I bet you were surprised."

"No doubt. I thought I was in for a paternity case, but she's an adult now."

"So she's Russian? That what those men were here about?"

"Something like that."

"What's Ivy think about that? You having a Russian daughter?"

"It's complicated."

Understanding that Irwin wasn't going to explain further, Mr. Hartshorne switched back to CNN. Before Irwin could retreat, his father-in-law turned from the TV to ask, "Is she good looking? Your Russian daughter?"

"Gorgeous."

"Ah." That could mean anything.

Irwin withdrew to the lanai. Baby Isaac might cry, but didn't require any explanations.

CHAPTER FOUR

Irwin still had hopes of keeping his family intact. "If I do move to Portland, will you come with me?"

Instead of a clear yes or no, she said, "We just drove all the way from Michigan in your old pickup. You know how far it is to Oregon?"

A truck was a truck. It was good for hauling fire wood but not for crossing the country. The Toyota was already old when he bought it, a Copper Country beater. They'd already had to replace the old snow tires and the fuel pump. "Maybe…"

She cut him off. "I already have a job. I start in a few weeks. You haven't even looked."

Well he had, sort of. Checked web sites for colleges and found none that offered Russian. He had seen Ivy's class schedule. Adjunct teaching jobs, no benefits, not even health insurance, not tenure track, were shit. "Your job isn't full time. You can't live on just a couple of German classes."

She countered, "But I'm rent free here."

"In a lanai? There's no heat and no privacy. It gets cold even in Florida. The neighbors don't like to hear babies crying. I can do us better than that."

She had to admit it was true. Being a single mom living with her parents and sleeping with their baby on what was just a screened in porch was a pretty minimal existence, even in Sunset Village. "You have a better idea?"

"Let's see what the FBI comes up with. It's time we took advantage of them instead of the other way around."

"You want to go under cover for the FBI?" Her face contorted like she'd tasted something foul.

Irwin was indecisive. A guy was supposed to take charge. He was always being exploited, taken advantage of.

"You wouldn't work for Vladimir."

Irwin had had that offer before, in Moscow, when Potinsky thought he had him caught in the honey pot trap. Irwin had wriggled out of that dilemma, but the result was a disaster. To actually be an employee of an ex-KGB colonel seemed to him to be a sell out for a good American even if Vladimir had been given political asylum and appeared to be legitimate. Yet, they were both fathers to the same daughter. It was an odd family arrangement, could be. It was family stuff.

"Maybe the FBI aren't really after Katja. If anything, they're after Vladimir. He stole all that Mafia money. He has connections. I'll bet he can't keep from getting involved with something criminal."

"Even if they come after him again to kill him?" It had happened once but Katja had intervened.

Ivy knew about Vladimir from their time at the Farm where the interrogation took place. It was an odd chapter in their lives, people never using their real names, innocuous conversations at lunch, all that secrecy. "I can't see him sitting on his hands in some retirement home and playing bridge."

"I wouldn't be a pole dance security guard, but maybe he'd have use for an office manager. He's got a ton of money."

Ivy smiled. "See? You're already half way to Portland."

Irwin wasn't ready to give up on their marriage. He also didn't want to be separated from Isaac. The baby was already crawling, would soon be walking, like Pinocchio said, a real boy. "If I did it and got a nice apartment, would you come with me? I heard Portland is a great place."

Too many ifs. If the FBI came up with an offer. If Katja really was a sleeper agent. If he got a job with Vladimir. If Ivy changed her mind. If, if, if.

CHAPTER FIVE

Dear Katja,

Yes, the FBI were here and claim you are not my real daughter, that the DNA test result was a fake. They want me to move to Portland. If they expect me to inform on you, it is a terrible idea. Parents informing on their children and children reporting on their parents-- that's police state stuff, a nightmare. What's in the family stays in the family. We, you, Ivy, baby Isaac, you are my family. Some things must be sacred.

I think the FBI believe you are a trained spy. Is that why you carry a gun? Have a concealed carry permit? You do not strike me as a second amendment gun nut. Please explain.

I do not suspect you, but Vladimir is another story. His natural instinct is to be KGB or GRU or whatever they call it nowadays. Maybe he is the FBI's real target.

All this mystery complicates your proposal that I move to Portland. It would be nice, in a perfect world, if I had a decent job and Ivy could be a stay at home mom for Isaac. Unfortunately, it is not a perfect world.

It's all very awkward. With all this, do you still want me to stay with you until I get settled?

Your American papa,

Irwin

Dear "papa" Irwin,

You did not need to know this before. It was all Vladimir's idea. He knew I wasn't his birth daughter. For a long time he wan angry at my mother. He put me in a boarding school. When my mother got cancer she told me about you. I was her accident, so I was not wanted. Then Vladimir decided he had a use for me. He always uses people.

Vladimir knew that the Russian Mafia would come after him for taking their money. He decided to move what he stole to an American account in my name, what you call laundering money. For my self defense, he also got me training in shooting and fighting. I am not Russian spy

Vladimir told me about you, that you are my birth father. He also said you are an honorable person. You refusing to work for the KGB told him you have courage and character. He knew if you learned that I was your daughter you would protect me. So he send me to America.

If Vladimir were as cold a person as you think, he would not care if we were in the same city in America. He could live anywhere. I do not think it is only because his money was in my bank account. Even if he is a reluctant Russian father, he has loyalty. He sees me as a Putinsky. So I am what you call a hyphenated person, Katja Putinrky-Glass or just Katie Glass in American language.

That makes us a strange family.

If you are still willing to move to Portland, you are welcome, my American papa.

Love,

Katja

CHAPTER SIX

For Ivy, nursing Isaac had become routine, nothing to be shy about, even though her mother complained about modesty. She read Katja's letter with Isaac on her lap, nursing at her right breast. It was a domestic scene, worthy of a Dutch painting, a young mother and her baby, except for the letter.

Irwin was anxious about her reaction. "What do you think?"

She handed back the letter and tended to Isaac. Time to change nipples. "I think anything to do with Vladimir Putinsky can be dangerous."

"Portland is a big city. We don't have to be his next door neighbors."

"Do my folks know about this?"

"I never told them. Your dad knows Katja is our daughter."

"Your daughter. Your maybe daughter."

"You know how they say 'only on a need to know basis.'"

She agreed, "Like they don't need to know about that business in our kitchen and Katja killing that guy."

"Definitely not that. Your folks would freak out."

Ivy wasn't so sure. "My Dad would think it exciting."

Reading thrillers was one thing. Reality was another. In the James Bond movies forty people might get killed, but nobody got hurt, nobody bled on your kitchen floor. The recollection made Irwin queasy. He had to hold his breath when cleaning up the blood. Having a yellow crime scene tape across your door wasn't fun. "Your dad wants me to go with him to the Kracker Koffee shop to tell his cronies about Katja."

Ivy laughed. "They'd eat it up along with their bacon and eggs. You know some of those old men are wise guys."

"Wise guys?"

"It's what old criminals on the witness protection program call themselves. Tell them about your exploit in Moscow and you'll be practically one of the gang."

"There's a thought. Maybe they'd know how to deal with Vladimir."

Ivy shook her head. "You're already talking like an old mobster yourself, Irwin. If they find out you were an FBI informant they might not be so friendly."

Irwin showed his empty palms to demonstrate his innocence. "Who, me?" If pressed, he would have to admit that working with the FBI had made him start thinking like a cop. His brain was altered by the activity. What you do changes you.

Little Isaac, having eaten, began to bear down. Time to change the diaper. Ivey had to attend to him. "You go ahead to the Kracker Koffee. Maybe you'll get some tips for when those FBI guys come back." She gave Irwin a close look. "You know the FBI. They will be back."

Well, why not?

Ivy followed with, "Do you believe her letter? That she is not a spy?"

Irwin shrugged. "I hope she is telling the truth."

The next day as Bill Hartshorne was getting ready for his morning walk to the coffee shop, Irwin intercepted him. "You asked about my Russian daughter. Here she is." He showed a winter photo of Katja in a snorkel storm jacket, holding the Russian teddy bear Irwin had given her. He wondered if she still had it or if it disappeared when she disappeared, too.

Bill Hartshorne studied the photo like a man who had not stopped looking a pretty girls. "Doesn't look like you."

"She has my nose."

"Bring the picture. I want to introduce you to the guys anyway."

They left Sunset Village, stepping out of the way for one of those golf carts. You never knew if the driver actually could see you or just pointed in a general direction and drove.

The summer had been dry, without the brief Florida downpours that quickly evaporated, intensifying the humidity and reactivating the mosquitoes. The summers were notorious for being buggy and muggy. Ocala, being inland, didn't enjoy Gulf or Atlantic breezes. Though it was still early, the lawns had no dew on them. Because of a water shortage, sprinkling was staggered and brief. If they all came on at once the pressure could sustain only trickles.

Irwin had never been inside the coffee shop. It was decorated with plastic oranges in a style which could be called Florida kitsch. A couple of fake stuffed marlins gathered dust on the wall above the counter alongside the posted menu full of items substituting the letter C for K.

The men at the regular table at Kracker Koffee were already there. They had to steal a chair from an adjoining table and shifted their own so they could make room for Irwin. The four old men all wore baseball caps and short sleeved sport shirts. One baseball cap was emblazoned 101st airborne, the second simply World War II, veterans of the so-called greatest generation. Two of the men's shirts were unbuttoned to expose cleavage with the telltale scars of open heart surgery, worn like a badge of honor or seniority. What was not exposed were the eyes of two of them, dark glasses like Secret Service watchers.

"This is my son-in-law Irwin." Bill Hartshorne introduced the men. "Mo, used to sell used cars in New

Jersey, Larry plays a lot of golf, Chuckie is the skinny guy you don't want o play poker with, and Mack. He doesn't say what he does or did."

Mack, silent, nodded. He was one of those in dark glasses. Chuckie didn't look up from his cup of coffee as if showing his face might reveal one of his tells. Larry was deeply tanned from too many hours on the course Mo said "Hyah" with the friendly but not necessarily sincere smile that went with pitching a used car.

Irwin tried to size them up. If two of these were so-called wise guys, which was it. He'd vote for Mack and Chuckie, but except for crime movies, Irwin had no idea what a gangster looked like. None wore shiny pin striped suits like John Ghatti. Sport shirts did not come with hundred dollar white silk ties. Since they were all sitting down, Irwin couldn't tell if under their shirt tails they carried FBI style heat. They were just a bunch of retirees having breakfast.

Was this what Irwin would look like in about twenty or thirty years? He was over forty now, and social security was just beyond the horizon.

Seated beside Irwin, Bill Hartshorne explained, "Irwin and our daughter Ivy have moved down from the Upper Peninsula of Michigan. They're staying with us along with our grandchild Isaac."

"Yeh, we seen the baby picture." Larry said, obviously bored with baby pictures of great grandchildren.

"In Sunset Village?" Mo asked. "I thought they didn't allow kids."

"It's only temporary," Irwin explained.

Bill couldn't wait for Irwin to get to his story. "Irwin has a Russian daughter. A looker. Show them the picture."

Irwin sighed and opened the envelope he carried with Katja picture with the Russian stuffed bear.

It was passed around the table to nods of appreciation. Larry had to wipe the bacon grease off his fingers with a paper napkin before touching the print. "How come you got a Russian daughter?"

57

Irwin was reluctant to get into it and vowed to say as little as possible. "A one night stand in Moscow twenty years ago."

Mack broke his silence and laughed sarcastically. "Some guys have all the luck. So did you get stuck with a paternity case?"

"I didn't find out until she was already eighteen."

Chuckie licked his lips and it wasn't because of the breakfast. "Looks like a nice piece of ass. No offense intended."

Irwin thought a man that ugly and old would find any willing woman was nice, but said nothing.

Bill Hartshorne was persistent in his desire for attention. "Katja carries a gun."

That got some raised eyebrows.

"Nine millimeter Glock," Irwin explained.

"Cop gun," Mack commented. "Standard issue. Used to be .38 Smith and Wessen revolvers, six shots, no fire power."

Chuckie added, "She got a concealed carry permit?"

They were interrupted by the waitress with the menus. She was in the far side of thirty and adept at dodging the butt pinches that inevitably came with the job of serving old letches.

Irwin pretended to study the laminated menu. He was looking for reactions. "The FBI think she's a Russian spy. A couple of agents came by the other day to ask questions." He turned to the waitress. "What's the special?"

She was bored. These guys were not generous tippers. "Scrambled eggs, bacon, hash browns. You want grits?"

In the UP of Michigan nobody knew grits.

Each of the men had a different reaction to the mention of the FBI, but Mack and Chuckie seemed to know. "Never lie to the FBI," Mack advised.

Chuckie agreed. "Lying to the FBI is a crime. You could get time in the joint. Like two weeks." The two men laughed.

Irwin didn't get the inside joke.

"If you confess and turn state's evidence," Mack explained.

Chuckie added "And don't get rubbed out first."

Irwin pleaded, "I've got nothing to hide."

Both of the old guys leaned back in their plastic, restaurant chairs and laughed. "Everybody's got something to hide."

If asked, Irwin had plenty to hide. Fortunately, nobody asked.

When they settled down, Mo asked, "Your Russian daughter ever use that gun?"

Reluctant, Irwin confessed. "She killed a guy."

Ah's all around.

Irwin hastily added. "Self defense. She wasn't charged."

Mo nodded like he knew. "It's always self defense. Like I was in fear of my life."

They had all heard that excuse before, usually from police killing African Americans. Florida had a stand your ground law. If someone was belligerent and you were afraid, just shoot them.

Bill Hartshorne hadn't heard that part of the story before, the part about the killing.. He asked Irwin, "Do you have a gun?"

Irwin didn't. He also concluded that if these wise guys were convicted felons in witness protection, they weren't allowed to own firearms, as if that mattered.

Chuckie patted Irwin on the shoulder. He handed back Katja's picture. "Stick with her, kid. She's your body guard."

Irwin hadn't thought of it that way. Katja his body guard? What? Against Vladimir? Could happen.

That was breakfast. When they got up to leave, having paid Dutch treat, Chuckie whispered to Irwin. "You don't need to lie to the feds, kid. Just don't tell them what they don't need to know. Never volunteer anything. Safer."

As they walked back to Sunset Village Bill asked, "She killed someone?"

Katja's photo was now safely back in the envelope. "You don't want to know."

Bill Hartshorne thought about it. "Maybe it's good that she's in Oregon."

Irwin rejoined Ivy in the lanai. She had set up her laptop on a folding card table and was working on lesson plans for the new job. She turned to him, "How was the breakfast?"

"They serve grits. Goes with being a Kracker place, I guess. You were right about the wise guys."

"Did you learn anything?"

"Only never to volunteer anything to the FBI unless they ask."

"Did you?"

"I regret it now. I mentioned Vladimir."

She shook her head. "Irwin, for all your business with that agent in Marquette you should know better. You're such a babe in the woods."

"It's part of my charm."

She gave him an unaccustomed warm look. "That's what I like about you, Mr. Glass. You're an innocent."

"If only. When do you think those FBI guys will be back?"

"My guess is as soon as they can make you an offer you can't refuse."

Irwin scratched his head. "Now you're sounding like the Godfather."

She chuckled, looked over her shoulder at Isaac snoozing in his crib on the floor. "FBI, wise guys, Vladimir and the KGB. Is there a difference?"

An offer he couldn't refuse. Irwin wondered what that would be.

CHAPTER SEVEN

This time the FBI visit was more formal. They came in a black Honda SUV and wore dark jackets, striped dress shirts and ties, one blue, one orange like the sports shirts they had worn before. Must be their favorite colors. When they came to the door to the Hartshorne's pre-manufactured home, also known as a trailer that could be jacked up and driven away on short notice, they didn't need to show their ID.

Irwin insisted. "I never got your names. I'm sure it's not Larry and Mo."

The one who he remembered had worn the blue shirt and was the most senior showed he had a sense of humor "Not Jack and Jill, either. I'm Agent Kirkwood and my partner here is Agent Rudy Romano."

"Romano, eh? I suppose you specialize in Italian Mafia cases."

Rudy Romano shook his head, perhaps regretfully. "Since the election it's all Russians."

Bill Hartshorne had not gotten up from his recliner, but he did turn off the TV. "I'm Irwin's father-in-law. at least for the time being."

Kirkwood raised his eyebrows. "Sounds like a temporary arrangement."

"Depends on my wife." Irwin called Ivy in from the lanai.

Isaac had been fussy so she hoisted him up out of his crib and carried him in on her hip. "Hello."

"These are agents..." Irwin began.

"I know, I heard."

Kirkwood looked around the living space, saw no privacy. "Where can we talk?"

"In the Lanai," Ivy suggested. "Anything you have to say to my husband I want to hear, too."

Irwin was pleasantly surprised that she said 'my husband.' She was defending her marital territory. A good sign.

"Don't mind me," Bill said, sinking back in his chair. The TV went back on as if automatically. CNN, a panel of people with opinions but not real news.

They withdrew to the Lanai.

They had only one patio chair and a folding chair Ivy was using while at her computer. The bed was an air mattress on a minimal frame, the sort of accommodation brought out for an occasional guest, then put away. The two agents could only sit on the unsteady mattress. They looked uncomfortable in their dark jackets and ties. Sitting on an air mattress that needed a bit more air was not very formal.

Irwin liked having the upper hand. He was like the executive who has the good chair and the visitors something that might give way under them and leave them struggling on the floor. It was a tactic familiar to the Chinese.

Ivy wasted no time. "So what are Agents Kirkwood and Romano here for this time?"

Kirkwood took the lead. "We're interested in Katja Putinsky."

Irwin corrected them. Katie Putinsky-Glass. My daughter,"

Romano wasn't going to take that bait. "What are your plans?"

"She wants me to stay with her in Portland until I get settled."

Kirkwood: "Settled meaning what?"

"In a situation so I can be together with my wife and our son."

Ivy wasn't so sure about that, but remembered the advice Irwin got from the wise guys at breakfast: never offer information unless the FBI asks for it. Their pending separation would only complicate the discussion, lead it off in a wrong direction.

Kirkwood asked, "What kind of situation?"

Before Irwin could come up with something, Ivy stated her terms. "A good, steady job, nice income, a decent apartment."

Kirkwood raised his eyebrows. He was obviously impressed. "You make your husband sound like a defector being setup with a new identity."

"Katja isn't a defector," Irwin put in. "She an American citizen now."

Romano nodded his appreciation. "You handled that well, Mr. Glass, seeing to it that she got citizenship."

Irwin didn't want to accept their assertion that the DNA sample was faked. "Since my paternity was proved, she was entitled, just any American who has a child born abroad."

Ivy was like a terrier not willing to give up a bone. "So what have you got to offer?" As if they had, which they had not.

Kirkwood wasn't intimidated. "It'll be better than a lanai with nothing but an air mattress and a beach chair."

"So?"

The two agents looked at each other. Romano shifted his precarious position on the air mattress. Kirkwood pursed his lips in thought. "That's above my pay grade. We'll have to talk to someone at a higher level and see what can be arranged."

"A contract we can sign," Ivy insisted.

The two agents got up to leave.

Ivy, carrying baby Isaac, made it a point to see them out, a mother, the alpha female, guarding her territory.

As they drove off, Irwin hugged her. "I'm impressed. From now on you do all the negotiation."

"If I let you do it they'd have you sleeping in the back of your truck on the street."

"Maybe you could ask them for a better vehicle."

She laughed. "Don't count on it."

"So you're willing to go to Oregon?"

She had to admit. "Did you see them squirming on that air mattress? Reminded me that we have to get something better. Like you said, it's time we took advantage of the FBI instead of them making you some patsy." A patsy? She was already talking like a mob wife.

"What do you think they'll come up with?"

"A counter offer. It's like buying a house, only we're trying to get them to do it.

Irwin laughed. "I have to admit you snookered them. They had no intention of offering anything at all."

"They still might not, but we planted the idea that they should." She looked around the lanai, assessed her situation. "I don't think this would be good for me and Isaac."

Irwin agreed but he didn't want to interfere with her ruminations.

She picked up the thought. "I admit that I was a little jealous of Katja. She's got a better figure than I have. She's mysterious. Having her in our household was anything but mundane."

"Like shooting an intended assassin."

Ivy shuddered at the recollection. "It's a good thing she was there."

Having Katja in their life was dramatic, mysterious, though somewhat sinister.

Ivy wasn't finished. "I didn't think jerking around in that pickup all the way to Florida was pleasant, but I have to admit it was kind of an adventure."

"Imagine what it might be like in Portland, Oregon. What should we tell Katja?"

"For now nothing."

They would have to wait and find out what Kirkwood and Romano came up with.

CHAPTER EIGHT

The parking rule at Sunset Village was only one vehicle per rented site and the Hartshornes' old Buick took it. Irwin had to leave his Toyota pickup in the guest parking lot along with several boats on trailers and two travel trailers that were streaked with dirt from the rains and were probably riddled with mold. Anything parked in that lot was an invitation to thieves that might steal outboard motors and the contents of any parked vehicle. The only thing of value in Irwin's Toyota might be the new set of tires, but they weren't a size most people could use. He had never had hub caps anyway.

All the way down from Upper Michigan with their stuff in the open bed of the truck they were afraid it would be rifled while they stayed in a motel. A permanent cover could at least be locked. Irwin checked the local classifieds for a box to mount over the truck bed. If he found a high one with side windows he could even use if for camping. In a pinch, with a mattress in it, he could sleep in the back of the truck if he actually did drive it to Oregon. It wasn't a pleasant option, but it would save motel costs. It was plan C. He didn't have a plan B. If he did sell the truck, having a box would be a good selling point.

Yielding to Ivy's advice, at first Irwin didn't write Katja about the possibility that the three of them would move to Oregon. What he didn't know was the Florida Department of Motor Vehicles had discovered a lucrative source of income. He was checking on the truck in the visitor's lot when he found a notice on the windshield. Florida law said that vehicles kept there long term, more than a month, had to be registered in the state. There was a tax.

When Irwin found the notice he looked up the regulations on the internet. He learned that if you were on the road a lot, one of those RV full timers who Gypsy-like traveled around the country and the national parks, it was beneficial to register a vehicle in Texas. Ah, but this was not Texas. The Florida economy depended on dollars milked from the tourists. So was he or wasn't he a long term visitor or a resident? He didn't know himself.

Irwin located the DMV office.

The clerk was unfriendly, a gray-haired man with a Col. Saunders beard, who had worked there for years and heard every story. DMV clerks are constantly hit with excuses and lies, that their driver's licenses should be reinstated, that the DUI was a mistake and expunged, that they should keep on driving even though elderly and half blind. etc.

Irwin was told if he was gong to be a resident of Florida, which he could be after one month, he would need a driver's license and Florida plates on the truck.

Irwin protested. "We're only visiting here."

The clerk's knowledge of their situation told Irwin that the surveillance state was well oiled. "Your forwarding address from Michigan is to Sunset Village. Your wife has a contract to teach here at the university. Sounds like long term residence to us, Mr. Glass. After a month you are a Florida resident. You should register to vote here, too. You can do that when you apply for a driver's license. "

Irwin remembered the wise guys at the Kracker Koffee. They were probably under the witness protection program with fake driver's licenses set up by the FBI. What would they say? So he bluffed, appealing to the clerk's view of himself as an insider. "Are you familiar with FBI agents Kirkwood and Romano?"

"Never heard of them."

Irwin took a guess. "They work out of the Tampa office. Mrs. Glass and I are here on what you might call a temporary assignment. We're awaiting transfer."

That was an excuse the clerk hadn't heard before.

Irwin leaned close to the counter and whispered. "Up in Michigan I was an FBI informant against some Arab terrorists. My cover was blown and we had to leave town."

"Kirkwood and Mozzarella you say?"

"Romano, different kind of cheese. But if you call them, don't say anything about the Michigan assignment. I'm not supposed to talk about it."

"We'll give you another month, Mr. Glass. Then you'll need a Florida license and plates for that truck."

Sounded like they'd have to make a decision soon. If not, Ivy's job would be starting and he might actually have to drive to Oregon alone and sleep in the back of that truck all the way.

CHAPTER NINE

Back from the DMV Irwin asked Ivy, "What should I tell Katja?"

"What? That you'll work for Vladimir Putinsky as a security guard at a strip club? As what? Someone to check on the girls' costumes?"

Irwin swallowed. "But they don't wear any."

"Lucky you."

"I heard Woody Allan had a job like that. When he stopped looking he quit."

Ivy smirked. "He's a letch."

"I'm not going to take a job like that."

"What about standing around in a shopping mall watching for shop lifters?"

Irwin shuddered at the thought. He couldn't imagine himself standing around in a fake uniform for hours. He'd rather be a greeter saying 'Welcome to Wal-Mart.'"

He remembered his job at Michigan Institute of Technology. "I don't want to teach bonehead English to foreign students. The FBI would want me to inform on them. Knowing the consequences, I couldn't stand that."

Ivy was impatient and testy. "Teach Russian history. You could do that. Apply. You can do that on the internet. Just whip up your resume. You don't have to mention being faculty advisor to the Moslem Student Association."

At least it couldn't do any harm. Irwin suspected that colleges got literally hundreds of applications for teaching jobs, hungry new-baked Ph.D.s desperate for a job, any teaching job, because the academic world was all they knew. He didn't have a Ph.D. A Masters wasn't good enough as a ticket to a job interview.

He did have a brief, practical background in International Relations, including what happens when the secret police seduce you and try blackmail. How could he put that in a resume? Applicant has experience of a honey pot seduction? Getting laid by the KGB was hardly a job qualification. Working at the American Library in Moscow was so long ago, did it count at all?

"I'll try." He got busy. At least doing job applications was something while waiting for Kirkwood and Romano to get off the pot. He'd send Katja a copy of the resume. She could shop it around at Portland State where she was enrolled.

He was depressed. He was out of a job, living on his in-law's screened in porch like some student, sleeping on an inflatable mattress and sharing a single bathroom as a barely tolerated guest.. At least he wasn't burdened by a massive, perpetual student loan. He had started from nothing when he got back from Russia, but that was years ago. He didn't have a wife then or a kid to be responsible for. Now he was starting over.

If Ivy dumped him, too, what was left?

Resigned, he sat down at that recycled manual typewriter and wrote Katja.

Dear Katja,

Here is a copy of my resume. Maybe Portland State can use someone who is Russian speaking and can teach Russian history. There are other colleges there-- University of Portland, CCC, and I guess another, Pacifica, in Forest Grove, wherever that is. Do you think a few calls could help?

If I could find a decent job Ivy and baby Isaac could be with me.

Ivy says maybe Vladimir might have something. I do not want to be a bouncer at a strip club or to stand around a shopping mall as a security guard who doesn't even carry a gun. Not that I'd know what to do with one. You know how I am about guns. But maybe Vladimir has come connections in Portland. You say there are five thousand Russians in Portland. Do you know anything about that? You need connections in this life.

I guess I was your connection when Vladimir sent you to the United States as my daughter. Now you can be mine.

If I come to Portland we'll need housing. I thank you for the invitation to sleep on your couch, but if Ivy and Isaac come with me, we'll need something more suitable. What is the situation there? How much is typical rent?

Everything is up in the air, but Florida authorities are looking at me like am a permanent resident, likely to register to vote and pay local taxes.

Please write soon.

Your American papa,

Irwin

Before he could get a reply, the two FBI agents showed up, again in the black SUV, so they weren't using the out of town temporary duty as a chance to rent a roadster and go to the beach. They wasted no time with informalities. It was early, so Bill Hartshorne was hanging out at Kracker Koffee with his pals. Mrs. Hartshorne had fired up their old Buick with a puff of smoke and was shopping for yarn. This time they could avoid sitting on the air mattress. They had the place to themselves but avoided the well-worn Lay-Z-Boy recliner. Isaac had his morning feed and spit-up, so was back in his crib for a snooze. They took positions at the dining room table.

Agent Kirkwood took the host dining room chair, the one with the arm rests, the power position. He carried a briefcase and produced a manila folder. Irwin could see their photos clipped to the cover. Kirkwood was making a little show of officialdom.

Ivy impatiently interrupted it. "So what have you got to offer?"

Romano, the lower ranked of the two agents, observed. He was obviously amused by Ivy's no-nonsense aggressive attitude. Others might be irritated by uppity women, but Romano's background was Italian in a world where women ruled.

Kirkwood cleared his throat, recovering. "I don't see that we have to offer you anything." It sounded like a labor negotiation, with management offering nothing and the union begging.

Ivy realized she hadn't buttoned her shirt after nursing Isaac, started to button it, then left her cleavage open. A woman has to use all the tools available to her. "We're offering Irwin's access to Vladimir Putinsky, a dangerous ex-Soviet police colonel. He and Irwin are co-parents to Katja who is also suspect of being a sleeper agent. Vladimir now runs a private security company. Our situation is ready made for valuable insights nobody else can provide."

"A private security company?"

"Rent a cop," Irwin added.

Kirkwood tried to play down the value of that. "So?"

While Irwin had languished over his submission of resumes to colleges, Ivy had her own thoughts. She explained. "Do you know what access a private security company has? Alarm systems. Burglar alarms. Locks. Safes. "

Kirkwood admitted that.

Ivy continued, pressing her point hard. "Putinsky as ex-KGB is essentially a criminal. He's a big time thief. Irwin says there are five thousand Russians in Portland. I'm sure not all are mere refugees. Putinsky has connections to the Russian Mafia that launders its money in the United States just in case the Russian president turns on them or is replaced with somebody honest." She didn't add that Vladimir had stolen a fortune from the Mafia and they'd happily kill him, that they'd tried once before.

Kirkwood had opened the file folder and, to win time to think, pretended to peruse the pages in it. Finally, he admitted, "I can see your point."

Irwin glanced at Agent Romano. Same orange tie today, different jacket. Romano was obviously enjoying this.

Ivy continued. "As you probably already know, Irwin speaks fluent Russian and at one time worked in the State Department in Moscow." She wasn't about to say Irwin was fired. You only told the necessary part of the truth.

Kirkwood nodded.

"So we-- Irwin-- are valuable assets."

Irwin was glad she said "we." She included herself. She had made up her mind without telling him, just to keep him in suspense, but divorce was off the table.

The FBI men nodded.

"But," Ivy went on, with a glance to Irwin, "our situation here in Ocala is less than ideal."

That was obvious.

"So what we want from you is a nice apartment in Portland, air fare for the three of us, business class, and maybe a job that makes a nice cover story."

"The government only flies coach," Romano said, falling for the trap.

"Alright. We'll accept coach."

Kirkwood folded the manila file. "You're asking a lot, Mrs. Glass."

Now, its mission accomplished, Ivy buttoned her nursing blouse. "My husband has been badly used by our government. It's only fair."

Kirkwood folded. "I'll talk to our superiors and draw up an agreement."

Ivy got up to signal the meeting was over. She reached over to seal the deal by shaking the hands of both agents while Irwin, dazzled by her display, just grinned.

As they drove off, Irwin held Ivy by her shoulders. "You did great. Bargaining for business class was brilliant. And the hand shake... I caught that."

"I wasn't going to take any shit from those guys. I think Agent Romano liked it, an offer they couldn't refuse." From the lanai they heard the sound of fussy Isaac waking up, needing a fresh diaper. "I'm the godmother."

At that moment Bill Hartshorne returned from Kracker Koffee. He sensed that he'd missed something. "I saw the FBI car driving off. What happened?"

Irwin smiled, a feeling of joy welling up, not just because Ivy had made a deal, but that she was going to be with him. "We're moving to Oregon."

Bill Hartshorne protested. "What about your job here?"

"It's a part time temporary position."

They had never considered camping in the Hartshornes' lanai anything but an interval. In the meantime, while they waited for a confirmation from the government, Irwin wrote Katja.

Dear Katja,

Tell Vladimir that we're moving to Portland and looking for work, possibly teaching Russian at one of the local colleges. I'd also like to learn more about the rent-a-cop business. I heard there are more private security people in the country than official police.

Let me know if you had any luck with Portland State.

I appreciate your offer to me as a couch surfer, but I will need to find something proper, maybe an apartment in your neighborhood. I looked up your address on Google World and see that there's a nice park and a street car all connected with the university.

Is anything available? Like maybe a two bedroom apartment? And what would it cost? Until I find a job, we'll have to be pretty frugal. I wouldn't want to put Isaac in Day Care, which costs more than many low level jobs pay.

We will not be driving from Ocala. It's too far and the Toyota is a tough prospect, traveling with a baby. You can't ride with a baby on your lap.

So much to think about and plan for.

Your American papa,

Love,

Irwin

CHAPTER TEN

Katja was looking forward to Irwin and Ivy's arrival and to meet her new baby brother. She arranged to borrow Vladimir Putinsky's black Cadillac SUV to pick them up at PDX. Katja didn't own a car herself. She didn't need one. Her apartment in the Avalon Arms on the South Park blocks was close to the streetcar and the PSU urban campus. Portland's Tri-met public transport was about the best in the nation, a model for other cities to emulate.

She could have taken the red line Max light rail to the airport to meet Irwin and Ivy, but knew traveling with a baby and baggage would be awkward. Irwin had explained that to get to Portland they would first have to be driven by Bill Hartshorne in his old Buick to Orlando and then take the United flight, with a layover, to Oregon. It would be a long day and tough with a baby. At least Isaac was being nursed, no complications with bottles and formula.

Katja parked the Caddy in the short stay garage and waited at the arrivals gate. She was in uniform. She was not working for her Russian father in his private security business, but had wrangled a part time job as a campus cop at Portland State University. An advantage was that PSU campus security, thanks to an incident that made it necessary, were armed. Though she had an open carry permit for her Glock, she didn't like to attract the attention of students who were skittish if they saw someone packing heat. Who wants to ask an armed coed for a date? The guys were intimidated.

Katja passed the security at PDX with no trouble even though she was not part of the Portland police or Homeland Security. Americans were getting used to seeing lots of police. United Flight 734 arrived late.

At last Irwin and Ivy emerged with the trickle of arriving passengers. Irwin was carrying the baby in a car seat, plus a carry-on bag. Ivy was laden, too, with a carry-on, purse, and a baby's kit with diapers, etc. They were exhausted, but the baby was asleep.

Irwin was surprised to see Katja in a uniform. She looked official and smart, but sexy. She had a full figure which would make wearing a bulletproof vest uncomfortable.

With a cry of "Papa!" Katja gave Irwin a hug, Russian bear style and kissed Ivy on both cheeks She looked down into the baby seat Irwin carried with Isaac. "Hello little brother," she said, giving him a warm smile. One was not supposed to frown at a baby. It made them nervous.

Ivy had not seen Katja since the incident at the Adat Israel synagogue and the shooting. She was uncertain. "He has two teeth," she said, making lame conversation.

Katja asked, "Are you nursing?".

Ivy nodded.

"Ouch. Do you have much baggage? Follow me."

.Katja led the little Glass family down to baggage pickup. While they waited at the turntable she explained, "I have Vladi's car, so we don't need to take the Max."

"What's with the uniform?" Irwin asked. "I didn't expect an armed escort."

"I am campus cop. Part time." She winked at Irwin "One of the airport cops asked what I was doing at PDX. I told him I was escorting FBI informant."

Irwin rolled his eyes. Reference to his problem at Michigan Tech wasn't that funny. "With Vladimir in the rent a cop racket and you a campus cop, I'm beginning to feel surrounded."

Ivy discreetly didn't mention the deal they'd made with the FBI to fly to Portland instead of driving that beater Toyota pickup. Portland was almost as far away from Florida as Alaska. Driving could have taken a week.

They crossed to the parking garage. It was nearly nine o'clock, not yet entirely dark, but a warm night. Portland had been having a heat wave all summer, many 90 degree days, and Oregonians, used to a wet Pacific climate, were ready to get out their rain jackets. Umbrellas were for sissies.

Irwin was surprised by the Cadillac. "That your car?" He knew Katja had access to the wealth Vladimir had stolen out of Russia, but the big, black SUV didn't fit the profile of a college student.

"Is Vladimir's. I have it for the weekend so you get settled."

Irwin, who had had to exchange tires on the Toyota, was curious about the Caddy's oversize wheels. When they opened the doors to get Isaac settled in the car seat, he commented, "This is built like a tank."

Katja smiled. "It is. You know Vladimir. H is paranoid. He wanted an armored car."

"I guess old habits die hard," Irwin said as he settled uneasily in the back seat with Ivy and Isaac. The front was fitted out like a patrol car with an on board computer monitor.

Ivy asked, "Did you find us someplace to stay? I guess we need a motel room until we find something."

Katja turned her head long enough for a quick smile. "I have surprise for you."

"Another surprise?" Irwin's voice sounded almost fearful.

They pulled out of the parking garage, blinked the lights at the gate, and passed through without stopping to pay the fee. Katja explained, "There is electronic thing under the license plate. When we pass the gate the bill is charged to Vladimir's account."

"Handy."

"Not just convenient," Katja explained. "It gives him a record of where the car was and what time."

They entered the freeway, merged with the traffic on the Banfield expressway. It was dusk. At that hour traffic was light.

Ivy asked, "What's the surprise?"

"Vladimir is acting like Mr. Mandeford before he went to prison. He laundered that mafia money through real estate. First he bought a luxury apartment in the Mirabella. Then he bought the apartment building where we are staying."

"All of us?"

"Katja laughed. "Vladimir is like those Pakistani motel owners. They use chain immigration. One buys an old motel and moves the family in as employees rent free. When they learn the business, they buy their own motels. Did you know forty percent of motels in America are owned by immigrants?"

Irwin remembered the motels they had stayed in on the trip down from Michigan. They all smelled of the same disinfectant.. "What's that got to do with Vladimir?"

Katja explained. "You and Ivy will be apartment house managers. Two thousand dollars a month and free apartment." It was the equivalent of almost fifty grand a year, adequate but not rich.

Irwin looked over his shoulder at Ivy. "That's convenient." He also quickly suspected that if he didn't want the job they would be homeless. They would be like the miners back in the Keweenaw part of Michigan's Upper Peninsula. Housing in the old days had been provided by the mine owners, as long as you worked for them. It was like owing your soul to the company store. To be evicted could mean freezing to death in the snow.

"It is two bedroom apartment on ground floor. It is high security building so you don't have to be door man. If there's toilet leak Vladimir has Ukrainian plumber."

Irwin thought about the arrangement. "I suppose the security guards he hires are Ukrainian, too."

"Some Russian. Good you speak the language, Papa."

"Maybe I should learn it, too," Ivy commented.

"No, but you could teach some of them English, like Irwin did at Michigan Tech."

That gave them all something to ponder as the heavy Cadillac left the freeway at the Sixth Avenue exit, headed for the South Park Blocks and the campus of Portland State University, a new phase in their lives..

CHAPTER ELEVEN

The spacious Avalon Arms parking garage was under the building on the South Park blocks. Though someone might sneak into the garage before the door closed, they couldn't get upstairs without swiping a magnetic key.

Before going up, Katja pointed out a bank of lockers secured with padlocks along the back wall. "Your is one of those for overflow things, like baggage, what there won't be room for in your apartment.."

It took two trips to get themselves, Isaac, and all their stuff inside the building. Katja gave Irwin and Ivy their hotel-like electronic keys to the ground floor apartment. The place looked new, or newly redecorated, a faint smell of recent paint. Irwin was impressed. Looking at his key which might have been for a credit card but had nothing but a registration number printed on it, he commented, "Looks like Vladimir takes his security seriously."

"It's a high crime neighborhood," was Katja's only explanation. Maybe that was a legitimate reason to carry a gun.

She let them in the apartment. "Make yourselves comfortable. There is some food in the refrigerator."

As Katja got ready to leave Irwin asked, "Where's your apartment?"

"On the fourth floor with a balcony. I'll show you later." Then she was gone.

The layout was modern and open, no dining room, but a counter with four high stools like a bar. Ivy went immediately to the freezer and was satisfied. Katja had been thoughtful. The freezer had a stack of frozen dinners, down below, fresh milk and a dozen extra large eggs. Bread in the cupboard. There was a bowl of pears, apples, and oranges on the counter.

Ivy was pleased to see the master bedroom had ample closet space. The smaller bedroom would be for Isaac. The bathroom had a shower, no tub, but double sinks.

What was different, because this was a concierge's apartment, was a porter's station in an alcove not much bigger than a walk-in closet. It could be closed off from the rest of the apartment so if someone walked up to the service window they couldn't look beyond. Above the service window, not visible from the hall, was a bank of monitors for the security cameras--front door, garage, and hallway where the mail boxes were built into the wall.

Irwin took a long look and closed the door behind him. "Vladimir does take his security seriously. The window for people to pass something in to the porter is bullet proof, like a bank."

"That's for you," Ivy said. She gave him a canny look. "You sure you want this?"

Irwin was suspicious. He knew Vladimir was not a man of charity or compassion. Irwin had been present for Vladimir's interviews at the Farm, Vladimir pleading fro political asylum. Was it just an act? That was little more than a year ago. In the time since Irwin had lost his job and Vladimir had moved to Portland and established himself. Though he and Vladimir were shared parents of Katja, he and Ivy were not like relatives of a Pakistani motel owner. Vladimir had to have an ulterior motive. Were they to be guests or prisoners?

When he'd got Katja's address he checked it out on Google World. It was choice: nice neighborhood, pleasant park, central location. If they had searched for a place on their own it might have to be in a distant suburb and require a month's rent in advance plus a security deposit. "The price is right. The cost of a modern two bedroom apartment in Portland is at least two thousand a month, even more. I checked."

It was all too convenient. This was Putinsky's territory. It made Irwin feel like a fly in the spider's web, held for some future lunch. If asked he would have to admit he was afraid of Vladimir Putinsky. Back in Moscow Vladimir had tried to control Irwin with sex photos. Now, living rent free made Irwin and Ivy beholden.

What was Putinsky's agenda? It might simply be a father seeing to it that Katja was supervised, like having her stay with a trustworthy uncle. But Irwin was not an uncle, and might not even be a relative if the FBI assertion was true, that the DNA sample was faked.

He didn't share those thoughts with Ivy. Their relationship, especially since Isaac was born, was complicated enough.

Ivy took off her shoes and flung herself down on the queen size bed. ""What I want is a nap. Good mattress." Her eyes were already glazing over.

Irwin didn't answer.

"What do you think?" Ivy asked, already half asleep.

Irwin was jet lagged, too. In Ocala it was already 1 AM. "I think I'd better talk to Vladimir."

"To see his fancy apartment?"

"That, too. But just what he's up to in Portland. I guess the FBI is interested. I have to check in with them, meet whoever's in charge."

"You going to spy on Vladimir Putinsky?"

"That fox? I'd feel like a field mouse encountering a rattler."

Ivy reminded him of their deal. "Just do enough to justify the government's moving expense and air fare they've paid to get us out here."

Irwin took off his shoes and lay down beside her. How much rest could they get before Isaac woke up wanting a change?

It didn't last.

CHAPTER TWELVE

Irwin was too tired to sleep. He tossed and turned trying to settle down. He would be seeing Vladimir Putinsky. He had met him only a couple of times, once in Moscow at the Astoria restaurant when Irwin was shown the photos of him having sex with who he now knew was Putinsky's wife and Katja's mother, and later in Gorky park when Irwin got cold feet and refused to be intimidated into spying against his own government.

The next time was when he and Ivy were called to the Farm outside Washington where Putinsky was being interrogated. He'd been negotiating for political asylum because the Russian Mafia were after him for revenge. He and Irwin carried on in Russian except for an embarrassing moment when Irwin asked why Mrs. Putinsky actually had intercourse with him when all she had to do was pose for the pictures. The response, in English, for the benefit of the watchers on the other side of the one way mirror was, "Because you had a nice cock."

Putinsky knew how to turn a conversation to his own advantage, a consummate manipulator.

Irwin and Ivy didn't know exactly the outcome of the interrogation, but now knew Vladimir had the asylum he requested and managed to keep the money he had hidden in

Katja's joint bank account, something Irwin hadn't discovered until the IRS wanted taxes on the interest.

It was an uneasy relationship between two men who didn't know each other but had a common daughter. That Vladimir had set up a new life in Portland didn't mean he was off the FBI's list. Agents Kirkwood and Romano had claimed Katja was a sleeper agent, but their real interest was Vladimir.

It was ironic. Twenty years ago in Moscow Putinsky had tried to recruit Irwin. Now in Portland he'd been working for him in a cooked up job as building manager. Vladimir had ruined his career with the State Department. Then the FBI snared him into reporting on the Moslem students at Michigan Institute of Technology with the result that two students died and his own reputation, what little there had been, was destroyed.

Twice he'd lost his job.

The Portland apartment and the new job-- were those two ways Putinsky was trying to make amends for the disaster in Russia? Seemed unlikely. Putinsky was KGB. Did such men have a conscience? A sense of loyalty? Guilt?

Or was Putinsky jealous of Katja's attachment to Irwin and Ivy and now an American baby brother Isaac? Was Irwin supposed to take over Putinsky's responsibilities as her Russian father? Katja didn't need a baby sitter.

She did need the parenting advice she could get from her American papa and stepmother.

It was awkward. Katja wasn't a little tyke. She had not grown up with Irwin being daddy. She was a svelte, sexy young woman Ivy plainly envied, even suggested, not entirely in jest, that Irwin should get a divorce from Ivy and take Katja, if the paternity proved to be bogus, as mistress or wife.

Maybe, Irwin mused, Ivy had consented to stay with him in Oregon to keep an eye on him. to watch over that relationship of American papa and sexy Russian maybe not daughter. . No matter how strained their relationship had been when they left Michigan, he was still her husband. There was that bond of ownership if not ideal partnership. They had sworn for sickness and health 'til death do you part.' There was that, too, if you took the marriage contract seriously.

No wonder he couldn't sleep.

Isaac woke up in the middle of the night, which it was, of course, on Florida time. A baby's cries are tuned to the mother. Even a lost lamb's cry is recognized by its mother in a flock of hundreds. Ivy reluctantly got out of bed, sleepily nursed and changed him into one of the last disposable diapers they had brought along. She had not bothered to undress, falling into bed so jet lagged and exhausted. She stripped to her underwear and joined Isaac in the spare bedroom's double bed.

In the morning, Irwin was still mulling over his situation. There was an advantage in moving from the Eastern time zone to Pacific. You picked up three hours of sleep, if you got over jet lag. Time to reset that internal clock.

Irwin rummaged around the kitchen, found a frying pan and a coffee maker, and started breakfast while Ivy got Isaac ready. Until they bought a high chair and a crib all they had for the baby was the car seat carrier. Ivy strapped it to one of the four stools at the bar.

"I didn't sleep worth a darn," Irwin complained. "I kept thinking that here I am again having to start out all over. And Putinsky! That bastard ruined what might have been a state department career, and now I'm to be working for him!"

Ivy accepted his offered plate of scrambled eggs and toast. "You'll bounce back."

"Then having to leave Michigan. I feel like a perpetual loser."

Ivy gave him a reassuring smile. "No you're not. You're a hero."

"I thought heroes were always winners."

"You're my hero."

Irwin was surprised. "How could I be your hero?"

"You're sticking with me even though I've been ready to split. That's loyalty."

"Maybe I'm just stubborn."

Ivy turned to Isaac who had discovered his fingers and was tasting them, like everything else. Dogs learn the world with their noses. Human babies discover the world through their mouths. "Do you think your Daddy is stubborn?"

Irwin was skeptical. "Maybe you're waiting for a better offer."

Ivy was stoic. "My father's cronies at Kracker Koffee say you play the hand you're dealt with, or...."

"Or what?"

"You cheat."

"I don't cheat."

"That makes you a hero, Irwin." She changed the subject. "When's Katja coming down?"

At that moment, she arrived.

Katja was in a pair of black short shorts and a patterned loose sleeveless shirt that provided no concealment if she was carrying her ever present weapon, but her stylish leather shoulder bag with buckles and pockets was heavy. Her short haircut for the hot Portland summer looked almost butch, but she was all girl. At least that was Irwin's impression. After years in Michigan's rustic Upper Peninsula he was not yet used to Portland which prided itself on being weird and had a prominent gay lesbian and trans community. What you saw wasn't necessary what you thought you got. Katja was sufficiently ambiguous to fit right in.

Irwin put out a cup of coffee for Katja who was interested in seeing Isaac at the breast. "What's it like to nurse a baby?"

Ivy didn't look up. "It's funny. The minute he was born, miracle! there was milk coming. A woman's hormones and her body change starting at the moment of conception."

"Do you feel like a different person?"

"It's strange. I am a mother now." Inexplicably, Ivy suddenly started to cry. "Sorry. I think it's post partum depression. Like maybe I wasn't ready. I didn't expect to change so much. Now it's too late."

"But you wanted to have a baby," Irwin said, almost accusing.

Turning the discussion to herself, Katja said, "I think I wanted to have a father, a real father, not a distant man in an office who sent me away to school."

It was hard for Irwin to grasp. He'd had a swell childhood in South Bend. Only his fixation on the Russian letter he found in the attic had changed his direction."

"Then I got you, my America papa."

She had put on that dark lipstick that reminded him of her mother, the encounter at the American Library in Moscow so many years before. It had been one of those imprinted images that never goes away.

"And we got you," Ivy commented after wiping her eyes. It was reassuring to have another female in the household. To share with. Her own mother was too engrossed in her hobby to be very sympathetic. Men didn't understand.

Irwin embraced the idea. "So here we are. What's next?"

"We're going shopping. I have Vladi's car for the weekend."

Ivy suggested, "Isaac needs diapers."

"Target."

Irwin added, "And a baby bed."

"IKEA." She explained both were near the airport.

"That's girl stuff," Irwin admitted, ready to bow out. Shopping wasn't his thing. "Maybe I'll stay here."

Ivy wouldn't have that. "As long as you can't feed Isaac, you're coming along as baby sitter."

Katja laughed. "Now you know what being a father is about."

He had never had to baby sit Katja. Then he remembered his mini-office as building manager. It had three closed circuit monitors. Using them, he would be able to see who came and went. If Katja brought a boyfriend in, that would be recorded. Were the monitors also connected to Putinsky's security firm office? Did this mean they were all under surveillance? Were there other, hidden cameras? It would be true to Vladimir's KGB mind set to do that.

There were other forms of fatherhood. Big daddy was watching.

CHAPTER THIRTEEN

Driving east over the Willamette River to Target for diapers in an armored car seemed strange. Of course, only a practiced eye would see the difference from an ordinary car. Maybe the multiple antennas on the roof were a giveaway. At Target Irwin was in charge of Isaac in the baby seat in one of the oversize shopping carts. While Ivy and Katja did their girl thing, he was baby sitter which he preferred to standing around the displays. Isaac was lively, waving his arms and legs and enjoying his body.

Irwin wasn't yet into baby clothes. Fatherhood doesn't hit a man in the way motherhood changes a woman. He parked himself in the snack bar and waited. When people saw the baby they stopped, asked about it, invoking his pride in fatherhood. He loved cuddling the baby in his arms to settle him down when he was fussy. Irwin stared lovingly into his son's eyes. Though infants can't talk, they can read your soul, feel the love, or, in worst cases, your resentment or irritation. Best to project only love.

When Isaac fell asleep, Irwin didn't want to put him down again. This was his cuddle. Cuddle was good. It was good to see a father holding a baby in public. Some men wouldn't do it, like it was undignified, unmanly.

On to Ikea at the other end of the shopping cluster that had grown up outside the airport. By then it was lunch time in the Ikea cafeteria, noisy with the weekend shopping crowd..

Ikea had delightful baby stuff, kids' cribs resembling a covered wagon, or a space ship, colorful patterns for sheets and blankets. The Swedes sure knew design even if they did have to find looms in India that could be the low bidders.

They had a lunch of Swedish meatballs, mashed potatoes and lingonberry sauce before loading up the back of the SUV with the heavy, flat packages which he would assemble later.

Once back in the apartment they had a nest building party setting up the nursery. Ikea had made a world wide success selling flat furniture, everything as a kit complete with Allen wrenches and, at the most, a screw driver. Irwin was delegated for the job of furniture assembly.

By the end of the afternoon it was all set up. They all had a sense of accomplishment. It was a happy moment of family building. He felt good.

Before Irwin had a face to face with Vladimir Putinsky, he would have to meet with the Portland FBI and find out what it was they wanted. Before he met with Vladimir about his responsibilities as building manager at the Avalon Arms he would want to know who else lived there. There were sixteen apartments, four on each floor. He had homework.

He made a list of the names on the mail boxes. Some were foreign, sounded Slavick maybe Russian or Ukrainian. A Kakievich couple were on the fourth floor. It made sense if Vladimir had connected with the Russian-speaking community. There were also a couple of Arabic names. Were they students? What students could afford such luxury living? Possibly Saudis.

He asked Katja, "Show me around the building."

Using his manager's pass key card, they called the elevator and went up to her apartment.

Katja's apartment was a one bedroom similar to his and Ivy's except instead of a porter's office it had an alcove she had set up as an office with her laptop and books, a tidy desk.

He recognized the stuffed bear he had given her back in Houghton. "You still have Ivan, your Russian bear."

She was pleased. "You remembered."

"Yes. He still wears the Red Star pin I took from my Russian winter hat." The first souvenir Americans bought when visiting Russia was a Russian fake fur winter hat with earflaps, easier to pack than a balalaika. .

What Irwin had not seen before were two framed photographs. One showed a young couple posing outside the Kremlin with a baby. It was a location Irwin remembered well from his first days in Moscow. The second was a glamour portrait of what had to be Katja's mother, Natasha.

Irwin gasped when he saw that one, the frank look, the generous mouth and the Slavic cheekbones. The resemblance to Katja was striking. The Mona Lisa had a smile people wondered about. In this case the smile said, "I know something you don't" A secret. No wonder when he looked closely at Katja he saw her mother's face and recalled that moment in the Metropole hotel room when she handed him a glass of vodka, made a toast, and dropped her red dress. It was the last he remembered before waking up on the cold street, drugged, and in just his Fruit of the Loom under shorts. Whenever he looked at Katja the memory blurred. Who was he looking at? His alleged daughter, or his nemesis? Holding the photo he said, "You never showed us this before."

"When my mother was dying she gave it to me."

Her expression told him there must be more to the story. "Did she know about me?"

Katja game him a look that said she knew more than she would tell. "She said you were the American. She said Vladimir demanded that she pose for his blackmail photographs. She wanted to get even with him."

Irwin got it, or thought he did. He remembered what Vladimir had said when they interrogated him at the Farm.

Why she actually had sex when all she needed was to pose for an incriminating picture. Vladimir had said because he had a "nice cock." Now he realized there was more to it than that. "She couldn't have known she'd get pregnant."

It was an awkward subject to discuss with a daughter he hardly new. They never talked about sex, but Katja was mature and worldly. He didn't know what private life she had before she turned up at his office and said he was her father.

Her explanation added a new dimension to that secret story. "She made him, what they call it? A cuckhold." She held up two fingers, the sign of the horns, Italian hand signal for cuckold.

Irwin could imagine. "Did he beat your mother?"

"She got a divorce." Katja took the framed photo from him and put it back in its place on her desk.

What other secrets did Katja have?

Katja changed the subject. "Let me show you the balcony." She opened the sliding glass doors. The balcony was just wide enough for a couple of green, plastic chairs and a little table..

They were at tree top level of the Park blocks. It was almost like living in the canopy of a forest. Portland, he had read, is thirty percent trees, a feature that makes it so different from other cities. The 5000 acre Forest Park creates miles of hiking trails inside the city limits. Irwin was not afraid of heights, but remembered how a favorite KGB method for assassination was to pitch a victim from a fourth floor window. He shuddered.

Down below between parallel streets, was the park with benches, people walking their dogs, a couple of homeless-men sitting beside their stolen grocery carts laden with their stuff. Straight down he could see the miniscule front lawn of the Avalon Arms and the ornamental iron gate, probably a necessity to prevent people from sleeping on the front steps.

"I have to make a phone call." He excused himself and took the elevator back down.

"She has a balcony," he told Ivy, "and some family photos. She still has that teddy bear I bought her, remember? Ivan?"

If Ivy thought their relationship was complicated and strained, at least infidelity wasn't part of it. He logged on to his laptop computer. He needed the phone number of the local FBI office. Fortunately, there was a card pinned on the concierge's notice board with the password for the wi-fi system.

He did not want to use the hard wired phone that came with the apartment. He was suspicious. The monitors above the service window and Vladimir's past as KGB worried him. He'd use his little track phone. He got the local FBI number off the web site and dialed.

"This is Irwin Glass. We just got in from Ocala, Florida at the convenience of the Florida office of the FBI. I need to make an appointment. When is a good time to come in?"

CHAPTER FOURTEEN

The office where Irwin was to meet his FBI Portland contact was in the government building. Katja could have dropped him off on her way to return Vladimir's car to the Mirabella, but he didn't want her to know where he was going. It was not very far away, a nice walk to orient him to downtown Portland and the Park Blocks. The government building had an all glass front, set back from the street and protected from potential Timothy McVeigh truck bombers by heavy posts. If a bomber did get in, the glass walls would be blown out without damage to the rest of the building. If was life in America in an a age of terrorism.

He had to pass three guards. He was wanded for possible weapons, had to take off his shoes and belt. It was higher security than they'd gone through at the airport.

Then he couldn't get into an elevator, had to ask for directions. He had to enter the floor he wanted on a key pad. One of the elevators would take him to that floor and none other. By the time he got to his destination he was half freaked out.

The security didn't end there. It was like getting into a fortress. He had to pass through a little vestibule with glass doors before he could talk to a receptionist, a young woman about thirty, blonde, modestly dressed in a blue, uniform style shirt with epaulets, no name tag, and, so far as he could tell, not armed.

The tall young man with a crew cut who came out to meet him was, just a sidearm, not the sort of hardware utility belt cops wore. "I'm Irwin Glass. I'm expected."

No introduction. At least the two agents he'd met in Ocala, Kirkwood and Romano, had names. "Come on in."

The interview room had a desk, visitor chair, a one way mirror reminiscent of where he had interrogated Potinsky at the Farm. On the table were three fat file folders.

Irwin asked, "Those my files?"

The no-name agent sniffed like he was catching a late summer cold. "Yours, Vladimir Putinsky, and Katja Vladovna Putinsky-Glass, alias Katie Glass."

Irwin imagined what was in those thick files. Maybe a record of all his conversations in Ocala. The agents there had a record of all his credit card purchases en route from Michigan and the motel bills. Maybe they had transcripts of all his phone calls. Depended on how thorough they were. "May I look?"

"In due time."

Irwin nodded. "Oh, I know: on a need to know basis."

No-name's head nodded minimally. "What I want to know is your history with your alleged daughter Katja."

"My birth daughter,": Irwin corrected, recalling the photo of Katja's mother. The resemblance was so strong he needed no documentation. "That's been settled."

"So you say. So when did you first meet her?"

"I was in my office at Michigan Institute of Technology in Houghton. She was out in the hallway and fingered me. In Russian she said, 'You're my father.' I guess that's every bachelor's nightmare. A one night stand and years later a confrontation."

"So what did you do?"

"Questioned her. She told me about her mother, that she had died of breast cancer, but told Katja she had a different father than Vladimir Putinsky."

"And you believed her?"

"Eventually we got a DNA test which turned out to be positive."

"Do you have a copy of the result?"

Now Irwin was getting irritated. "I'm sure you have it in that file. The important point was that since she was proved to be my birth daughter, daughter of a US citizen, she was entitled to US citizenship and a US passport, which she got."

No name was skeptical. "All on the basis of the DNA test?"

"I think they call it prima fascia evidence. It changed her birth certificate."

No name shifted to another topic. "What about this shooting in the kitchen of your rental house in Houghton?"

Irwin scratched his head. "Ivy and I--Ivy, that's my wife--wondered why Katja always carried a hand gun. That's not normal unless you're a paranoid gun nut or in some branch of law enforcement. But I knew her Russian father was a KGB officer, so maybe that was the connection. I didn't pry. We were discreet."

"So what happened?"

"We had a home invasion. A would be assassin broke in the kitchen door with a gun but before he could get his bearings Katja shot him. Blew his brains out. Blood all over the kitchen linoleum."

"She shot him, just like that?"

"Like she'd been trained." Irwin took a deep breath, remembering. "You understand we were in shock."

"You called the police?"

"Sure. No ID. The dead guy carried a Russian army issue pistol. He was clearly foreign by his clothes. It was self defense. Home invaders can be killed. It's an occupational hazard, I guess."

No name didn't think Irwin's quip was funny. "So she wasn't charged."

"Nope. When the crime scene tape was taken down I cleaned the floor with bleach. My hands smelled for days afterwards."

No name was leafing through the papers in the file. "There was another shooting. What was that about?"

Irwin tried to recall the scene, the synagogue party, latkes being fried in the kitchen, then the flash of light and flame. "We were at a Hanukah party in the assembly room at the Adat Israel synagogue in Hancock, Michigan. A Molotov cocktail fire bomb was tossed in. Katja ran out of the building in pursuit of the kid who threw it, fired one shot. She said she hit him in the thigh."

"That's not usually fatal."

"He slipped in the snow and fell into the path of a logging truck. He was crushed beyond recognition. How did you know he was shot? I didn't think there was an autopsy."

No explanation. "So she wasn't charged with discharging a firearm in the city limits?"

Irwin hadn't thought about that. "Adat Israel isn't in the city. Just outside. I guess that's a jurisdiction issue--city police versus county sheriff. Anyway, she was in hot pursuit, I think they call it. The kid had a university ID, a Palestinian foreign student."

He didn't want to get into why a Palestinian had been persuaded by a couple of the Arab students to torch the synagogue, as if a Northern Michigan synagogue had anything to do with hatred of Israel. He certainly didn't want to mention his report to the Marquette FBI agent Wilson and his fear that the report lead to the interdiction of the two students. That would only lead to more questions, more bad dreams including his awful meeting with the distraught parents. His guilty conscience was too painful. Too many consequences.

No Name turned more pages. "So now Katja's enrolled at Portland State University and has a part time job as a campus cop."

Irwin sighed. "That's the story. What else have you got?" He hoped nothing, but he was curious.

He was shown a document. "This is a copy of her original Russian birth certificate. We also have her gymnasium diploma." He pronounced the word American style as if it began with a j not a g. "We also have a copy of a certificate of marksmanship from a Russian government shooting range."

Irwin was surprised. "How did you get that?"

"The I in FBI stands for Investigation." Some things you don't ask.

No Name continued. "We think that marksmanship was part of her training at spy school." He gave Irwin a hard look. "That's where they learn how to kill somebody in seconds with their bare hands."

Irwin suppressed a shudder. He thought about her fingernails with that red polish. He couldn't imagine Katja killing anybody with her bare hands.

The FBI also had a copy of her application for a student visa and immigration's photos of her Russian passport taken when she entered the country at New York City. The FBI file even had the chest X-ray she'd had to have taken for fear of bringing in TB from Russia.

The agent did some back tracking. "There was something about income tax on a very big savings account. What was that about?"

"Katja disappeared, just took off. We didn't know to where. I opened a letter from the IRS, checked and found my name was also on the account. I think Putinsky set it up when he thought I'd work for the Russians, then saved it for his own purposes. I assumed this was money from Putinsky, so to force Katja to contact me, I moved the money to my personal account and paid the tax. Without access to cash, I hoped she'd come back home. She did."

"How much money was it?"

Irwin couldn't remember. "Vladimir Putinsky obviously used his KGB resources to steal a ton of money from the Russian Mafia, which is why he had to flee the country. They want him dead."

"That explains the home invader."

"I guess so." Irwin remembered what Katja had said about Vladimir, that he bought a condo in the Mirabella, a luxury apartment building, set himself up with a rent-a-cop security business, and even bought the Avalon Arms where Katja and now he and Ivy lived. This was how the Oligarchs laundered their money. How much did the man have, anyway?

The agent was interested in the home invasion. "So she shot him, just like that?"

Irwin nodded. He didn't want to remember the scene.

"And she was never charged?"

"No."

"If she had been, she couldn't buy a firearm, certainly couldn't have a concealed carry permit."

Irwin didn't know the rules on applications for weapons permits. He was beginning to feel hemmed in.

"You say she sometimes disappeared."

"Yes."

"Know where she went?"

"No idea."

"Maybe your fake daughter is mentally unstable. Ever thought of that?"

Irwin hadn't. He had chalked it up to teenager's sometimes rebellion.

No Name gathered the papers together and returned them to the folder. "We think your alleged daughter is a Russian sleeper agent and you are her cover. She may have been somewhere on assignment. We also think the paternity business is a made up story, a legend to get her an American father and an American passport. With Katja here as his daughter Putinsky could then come into the country as a chain migrant. A daughter can sponsor a father."

Irwin didn't want to believe that part. "But I'm her father--co-father." He clung to his version of the story. When you share your home with a real person, an FBI file isn't as real as intimate underwear hanging in your bathtub. Katja was part of their family. You can't imagine your kid is a Russian spy. Spies were not his world in spite of Putinsky's attempt to recruit him so many years ago.

No Name shook his head in disbelief. "Mr. Glass, either you are being very clever or you're a naïve simpleton."

Irwin didn't know whether he should be flattered or insulted. "Take your choice."

No Name chuckled. So he had a sense of humor after all. "There's no law against being a naïve simpleton. Knowingly harboring a foreign agent could make you a co-conspirator. Moving that money was money laundering. That's a crime, too."

He hadn't laundered any money. He had moved it to another account under his name. Irwin disagreed but decided not to say anything. No point to arguing with the FBI. Having a sleeper account in a foreign bank must be like having a spare passport just in case, something put aside for a rainy day. Vladimir had added Katja's name to it, then made a transfer. "What else do you have? What about Vladimir Putinsky?"

CHAPTER FIFTEEN

Agent No Name moved to the second file on the interview desk, Vladimir Putinsky's. This was not as fat as Katja's, perhaps because getting files out of Russia might not be as easy. Irwin could see the first page with a photo of Vladimir in a Russian uniform. He was younger then. "We know that Vladimir Putinsky, sometimes Putin, was a KGB officer. He used his own wife in any number of rogue honey pot setups. She would pose for sex photos which Putinsky used to blackmail his subjects into working for him. The difference was in addition to entrapping foreign diplomats, he went after Russian oligarchs. It was his own sideline. That was probably why he used his wife and not one of the KGB stable of prostitutes. Except in one case, his wife got pregnant. "

So he was in a sense pimping his own wife as a porn star. Nice guy. "That's my daughter, Katja," Irwin insisted, not wanting to let go of his story.

"That connection isn't certain. The daughter was sent to a government school and may have been substituted for a girl trained for the mission to claim you as the father."

"And Putinsky?"

No Name looked across the table at Irwin. "You know the rest from the interrogation at the Farm. Putinsky fled after stealing perhaps several million and stashing it in various offshore accounts and at least one with your name on it. Plus Katja's. She's part of his entrée to the United States. She's his insurance policy, and you."

"Me?"

No Name shook his head. "I think I'm going with naïve simpleton. Why do you think we were willing to fund your move from Florida to Portland? We want you on the inside."

That hurt. "You want me to inform on my daughter? What are you people? This isn't East Germany."

Now it made sense.

"You informed on the Moslem students back in Michigan."

That hurt. "Yes, and two of them are dead. It wasn't my fault. Someone misunderstood my report. It was all innocuous."

No Name wasn't going to have to open the third folder. That was Irwin's case file.

"You can cooperate, Mr. Glass, or you can be charged with harboring a foreign agent."

"But she hasn't done anything."

"Not yet, that we know of." He smirked. "Except for a couple of cases of manslaughter."

What was likely to happen? Would Katja be interdicted like those poor Arab students? Taken to Rumania or Bulgaria and tortured to death? "What if I refuse?"

"You can take your chances. I'd advise you to cooperate. We want to know what Putinsky is up to in Portland. Find out. Or is he your friend, too?"

"Vladimir is not my friend. He ruined my state department career."

"See?" No Name stood up. "You can reach me at this number." He handed over a business card.

Now Irwin had a name. FBI agent Martin Burke. Was that also an invention?

Putinsky was certainly not his friend, even if they shared fatherhood with Katja. Being employed as Putinsky's building manager for the Avalon Arms only made it more complicated. It made him captive to whatever schemes Putinsky was involved in. The apartment building could be legitimate, one of those ways criminals put a legal face on family business.

He also didn't want Putinsky for an enemy.

It was enough to put him in a state of bewilderment and confusion, between a rock and a hard place. Which was the rock? .

On his walk down to the government building on Second Avenue Irwin hadn't bothered to look back to recognize where he was coming from. He actually found himself lost. He was smart enough not to do the guy thing and not ask directions.

At last he was in front of the Avalon Arms. He had never entered the front door before, had only come in through the garage. Now he couldn't remember the key code for the entrance and felt foolish. Maybe Agent Burke was right: he was a simpleton. He had to use the intercom to call Ivy.

She took a long time to answer. Might be nursing Isaac. Finally she responded.

Irwin waved at the surveillance camera. "Let me in. I forgot the code."

At least he had the apartment door key card. When he got into the apartment, the first thing he said was, "Is there any coffee left?"

Ivy read his worried expression. "What happened at the FBI?"

He settled at the counter and sighed, held the cup with both hands and stared into it like there might be an answer down in the coffee.. "I was given an ultimatum. Cooperate or else."

Ivy was holding Isaac to her shoulder to burp him. "Or else what?"

"Or prosecute me--us--for harboring an agent of a foreign country."

"Katja?"

"Who else? Maybe they also think we smuggle microfilm in Isaac's diaper."

As if in response Isaac started to bear down. In one end, out the other. Time for a change. It wasn't microfilm.

Irwin followed Ivy into the nursery where they had an Ikea baby changing table.

While Ivy held Isaac's feet up so she could wipe his bottom she commented, "So they really do think she's a sleeper agent?"

"Some people are so suspicious they'll doubt it if you say it's raining in Portland. More important, I think the FBI is mainly interested in Vladimir. And I'm curious about all the people he has rented to in this building. It's a good front." The Avalon Arms might serve as a stable for a nest of foreign agents. He recalled the roster of tenants he had not yet met like the Kakievich couple. As building manager he would have rights to inspect all the apartments without a warrant. The FBI would like that. "This place is full of foreigners."

"So is the United States. When are you going to talk to Vladimir?"

CHAPTER SIXTEEN

"As soon as Katja gets back she can tell us where to find him."

While he waited, Irwin went over the list of tenants. A file drawer in the concierge's tiny office held a record of the renters along with their renter's agreements. The Avalon Arms was upscale, the rent on a two bedroom over two thousand a month, plus a damage deposit and a month's rent in advance. This was not a cheap student rental. Even faculty could hardly afford it, considering that half the PSU teaching staff were adjunct. That explained why none of the tenants were African-American. Few could afford the rent. Who could?

Maybe a kid of a Chinese millionaire. There were two Chinese but no Japanese names on the list of tenants. With a shudder of bad memory he recognized a couple of Arabic names. Whatever developed, he did not want a repeat of what happened back in Michigan.

When he took a break for lunch, he was reminded they needed to get some groceries. Man does not live on grilled cheese sandwiches alone.

Ivy had already figured it out. They could order groceries on line from Safeway and it would be delivered. That was convenient since they didn't have a car. Bill

Hartshorne had sold the pickup to one of his cronies at the Kracker Koffee. Five hundred bucks, if Bill Hartshorne sent it and didn't keep it as rent on the lanai, was hardly a down payment on something for Portland. Irwin wondered who had bought his Toyota. The two old vets had to be about ninety, but the wise guys were younger, could still drive, though in Florida there seemed to be no age limit on driving..

Irwin was troubled and asked Ivy for advice. "What do you think we should do about Katja?"

Ivy's eyes opened wide, like what?? "She already knows the FBI thinks she's a Russian spy. Didn't you say something about that in one of your letters? What if she says she is? What do you do then? Turn her in?"

"I don't think she's a spy."

"She must think you're in cahoots with the FBI."

"Just because they interviewed me doesn't mean I'm in cahoots."

Ivy laughed. "You told me that FBI guy thinks you are a simpleton."

Irwin felt sheepish. "I'd settle for dumbass."

"So?"

"I told Agent Burke I would not be an informant on my own daughter. I wasn't honest with the Moslem students and look what came of it. Dead."

"You weren't dishonest. You just didn't tell them you were watching them."

"That FBI guy suggested that Katja might be mentally unstable."

"What? Schizophrenic? He's jerking your chain, Irwin, planting seeds in our head."

It was like psychological warfare, the interrogator throwing him off balance. Irwin felt frustrated and taken advantage of. It was intolerable. "What should we do? Move out? Move back to the U.P.?" The thought of another seven month Keweenaw winter was chilling. That bridge was burned.

Ivy put his plate in the dishwasher. It was a nice apartment. Everything was new. They had just furnished Isaac's baby space with a bunch of furniture. They now had credit card debt. "I like this place. You don' t yet have a job at the university. You haven't talked with Vladimir. Maybe it's all legitimate. Maybe the FBI is just blowing smoke."

Katja showed up in the afternoon. Her dark lipstick conflicted with the uniform. She was wearing her PSU Campus Cop uniform and had a "don't mess with me" look. It must be something that happens whenever people put on policeman's garb. Like Superman putting on his cape or Harry Potter knowing his cape of invisibility makes him invulnerable. It was hard to imagine her as a Russian sleeper spy. What did a sleeper spy look like, anyway? Something in Mad magazine?

Irwin commented, "You look pretty dangerous in that uniform, too dangerous for a welcome hug."

She laughed and put her arms around him. Her sidearm dug into his hip. When they separated he said, "I need to get in touch with Vladimir. How do I do that?"

She gave him the a couple of numbers. "This is his apartment, this his office. He'll be at work now."

Using the hard wired land line, Irwin called the office number.

A female voice answered, "Security."

"This is Irwin Glass. I need to talk to Vladimir."

He was put through and got a Russian welcome, "*Tovarish!* Welcome to Portland. How do you like your apartment?"

Tovarish, comrade, didn't that go out when the Soviet Union collapsed? Was that an old habit or was Vladimir pulling his leg? "Very nice. Ivy loves it. When can I see you? I need to know what you expect of a building manager."

"Come to dinner at the Mirabella."

"Shall I bring Ivy and the baby?"

Vladimir had forgotten they now had a son. "Katja can be baby sit for a couple of hours."

"How do I get there?" Secretly he would like to be picked up in that armored Cadillac like some VIP. No luck. Vladimir was a boss, not a chauffeur.

"Katja will explain. Come at five thirty and we can tour the building." It was more of an order than an invitation. Before Irwin could agree, Putinsky hung up.

Katja explained that all they had to do was take the OHSU south bound streetcar and get off at the waterfront hospital The Mirabella was in the next block.

While Katja went up to her apartment to change out of her uniform Ivy did some Google research on her laptop. The Mirabella turned out to be a classy high rise apartment building on Portland's South Waterfront. It was somewhat airfoil shaped and offered views of the Willamette River and downtown Portland.

It was also expensive. Residents bought their condos, paid a hefty monthly maintenance fee, could resell the apartments or they could be part of their estates. The catch was they could not sell them for more than they paid in the first place, a means of preventing real estate speculators. It was a rich man's retirement.

"If we're going to dinner in that fancy restaurant," Ivy pointed out, showing the photo on the web pages, "I don't have anything to wear. All I have is Yooper clothes." Her pre-baby dresses no longer fit. In Northern Michigan's seven month winter women wore heavy slacks and snow boots. Dresses were an anachronism.   The shorts suitable for Sunset Village in Ocala were hardly suitable.

"Maybe Katja can lend you something." Though Ivy had not fully recovered her slender pre-baby shape, Katja's hips were wider.

Ivy did have one maternity skirt, something she didn't plan to ever need again. How complicated life got when you had a baby. Different body, different wardrobe, new routines. "I'll have to pump some milk for Isaac."

Once their logistics were settled they stepped out the front door of the Avalon Arms into the park and found the streetcar. They were not familiar with the system. One was supposed to buy tickets from the machine on the platform, a puzzle in itself. Then when they did board, they realized most people didn't pay at all. It was on the honor system. You took your chances on a fare inspector.

Thanks to Ivy's Internet research they had no trouble finding the Mirabella. It was imposing. One could walk in, but not beyond the reception desk. Because of security Vladimir had to come down to meet them.

Irwin had not seen Vladimir Putinsky in a long time, not since the interrogation at the Farm outside Washington. Even then it was across an interrogation table. At the Mirabella the Putinsky who emerged from the secure elevator was now completely bald, wore rimless spectacles and an unaccustomed smile that didn't reach his eyes. At about five foot six he was shorter than Irwin remembered. He wore dark blue slacks and a leather vest, reminiscent of the jacket Irwin did remember from the brief encounter at the American Library in Moscow. He guessed that standard KGB garb was either a long black overcoat or a leather jacket.

Putinsky dispensed with an American style handshake and embraced Irwin, air kissed him on both cheeks like the kiss of death. "Irvin!" he addressed his visitor with false camaraderie, unable to pronounce the W in Irwin. "*Kakpushevaika.*"

"*Horoshaw*, very well. This is Ivy."

Putinsky did not know Ivy, so no hug, just a respectful nod. "Do you also speak Russian?" He was sizing her up, too.

Ivy's eyes moved quickly as she studied their landlord, Irwin's old nemesis, Katja's Russian father. "German."

"*Ist auch gut*," Putinsky said, demonstrating his linguistic ability. "Let us first tour the building and then dinner."

The Mirabella was posh. There was a pool, exercise room, two restaurants, and on a lower floor a rehab center staffed with nursing students. The dining room was up top, views of the river with its many bridges and the Portland skyscrapers. City planners were trying to emulate Vancouver BC with its small footprint high rises to avoid the treeless canyon effect of New York.

A waiter brought the menu for the day. It showed no prices so Irwin guessed they had a meal plan.. Putinsky cautioned no business or politics at dinner. Irwin chose the steak and Ivy the salmon. Salad was mixed greens with pecans and a vinaigrette dressing. Dessert some kind of mousse. They both took a pass on the wine.

"No matter," Putinsky said. "I have vodka in my apartment."

Was that his standard operating procedure or just old Russian habits? The last vodka Irwin had drunk was in the bedroom in the Metropole in Moscow when Putinsky's wife dropped her red party dress and he passed out. No thanks.

They retired to Putinsky's tenth floor condo. Though it had only one bedroom it was spacious with a north-facing wall of windows. Oddly, Putinsky's choice of furniture was Ethan Allan in dark woods, a contrast to a sectional sofa in brown suede leather. This was not Ikea land.

Putinsky got out a bottle of Smirnov and plain water glasses. He offered some vodka to Ivy who explained, "I'm nursing. I don't want my baby to be a drunk." Irwin refused.

Finally they got down to business.

Irwin asked, "How's the rent-a-cop business?"

"It is not the same as in Russia," their host apologized. "We cannot arrest people. But I am hoping to have the men deputized. Oh, and the women, too." A nod to Ivy, "I have several women."

Before Irwin could ask for details, Putinsky added, "I am also in the home help business. I bought the Kirov agency."

Irwin made a mental note. He would have to look it up.

"It was owned by two brothers. One was in Los Angeles, the other in Portland. The Portland brother was murdered by some old lady."

"Sounds like quite a story," Ivy commented.

"Something about Medicare fraud and a fake clinic. I bought only the home helper franchise."

Ivy asked about that.

"We employ home helpers. Minimum two hour visits. Fifty dollars. Medicare pays."

"Where do you get the helpers?"

"We train them. Immigrants."

Ivy understood. "When you first come to a country all you can do is service jobs, like drive a cab, wash dishes, or go into home help."

Irwin could see an opportunity. "You teach them English?"

Vladimir smiled. "You could do that."

Irwin wasn't sure he wanted to do bonehead English, but it depended on who the immigrants were. The FBI would be interested. Did Putinsky hire Russian and Ukrainian immigrants? Or were they Mexican or central American? He didn't know Spanish. He thought the home invader Katja shot had been a Ukrainian.

It sounded like Putinsky lived near the edge of legal, no surprises if he operated on laundered Mafia money.

Irwin was reminded of Bill Hartshorne's wise guys. If they could stick to their new identities they were ex-gangsters. They were protected because they had come over to the law and order side to testify. Witness protection was to save their skins, but they also decided to serve the police. Did that make a wise guy a good guy?

And what was Vladimir Putinsky? Ex-KGB or gangster? What was the difference between a KGB government murderer or a mere hit man for the mob? Irwin didn't know if Vladimir had actually killed anybody. A colonel had flunkies for wet work.

That he and Vladimir were co-fathers of Katja only made the situation more complicated.

Ivy asked, "Why did you fix us up as building managers?"

Putinsky raised his nearly hairless eyebrows. "Why for you to keep an eye on Katja, of course. Our daughter. We can't have her going around shooting people."

Ouch. That hurt. Irwin commented, "Just so she doesn't get into patricide." He was thinking of himself.

"Patricide?" Putinsky didn't know that word.

"Killing your own father."

Putinsky's expression suggested he wasn't so sure about that. Maybe there was something to Agent Burke's suggestion of mental instability.

So far Irwin and Ivy thought of Katja only as a somehow trained sharpshooter. They didn't think the would turn her Glock on them. Would she? What would it take? She seemed stable and affectionate, but if she were schizophrenic, she could be dangerous.

Suddenly Ivy touched her breast, embarrassed. "Baby's calling." She smiled, almost shy. "It's like clockwork. When baby is hungry, milk comes. We have to go."

Putinsky made a perfunctory, insincere offer. "Shall I drive you?"

"The tram stops right across the street and goes to the Park Blocks."

CHAPTER SEVENTEEN

Having no experience with babies, Katja hadn't managed well with Isaac's diaper. She had, at least, fed him the few ounces of mother's milk Ivy had pumped off into a bottle, but it was not enough. He was still hungry. If they were to do this again, Katja would need some instructions. Babies didn't come with operator's manuals.

Irwin was already practiced and left Ivy with Isaac to satisfy Katja's curiosity about nursing. It was mother stuff. He retired to the concierge's mini-office to get more familiar with his made up job. There was more to it than just collecting the rents. He would also be janitor and doer of all things. He would have to get the trash out to the street in the specified containers. He had noticed the containers in the garage near the elevator. Portland not only recycled, but also collected compost. Then there was the stair well, four floors that had to be swept. Maybe he could give one of the student residents a break on the rent in exchange for some of those chores.

Who would that be? Not the Chinese, scions of the wealthy, or the Saudis, used to having servants do everything for them. Besides Kakievich there was one couple with a Slavic name, Russian or Possibly Ukrainian. All but one of the sixteen apartments were occupied, all on a renewable month to month basis, no binding year long leases. .

It was a professional step down from his teaching job at Michigan Institute of Technology. So was stepping down from a state department job in Russia to teaching Yooper Finnbilly freshmen at Michigan Institute of Technology. He'd had hopes of a foreign service career. Now he was to be little more than a janitor for a Russian criminal. When would he ever rise to his level of competence? Was this it? It was discouraging.

He remembered what Putinsky said about the home health agency. Bought from someone named Kirov. There must be something about that murder in the Oregonian.

Google pointed to a lot of Kirovs but finally he found it. The newspaper story told it all in a couple of sentences. Alexy Kirov, owner of a Portland home health agency, a clinic on Barbur boulevard and a durable medical supply store, had been shot by Mary Higgins, an elderly woman living at the Rose Plaza retirement complex. The clinic had been a front for Medicare fraud, had purchased Medicare numbers from gullible elderly people and used those to order durable medical equipment that was not needed and sometimes never used, if delivered. The clinic and the supply store were shut down, but the home health agency seemed to be legitimate.

Kirov had been attempting to murder an elderly resident but was prevented by Mrs. Higgins who still owned a World War II service revolver her late husband had given her, as she said, "In case Jerry came."

That was it, a human drama that got only a three inch story on a back page, less important than a high school sporting event. So much for life. The local TV must have had lurid coverage, typical interview of the heroic pensioner, but was that footage archived for public access?

So now Putinsky owned the home health business, too. Was it legitimate or, like Kirov's other businesses, shady? That might be of interest to Agent Burke.

Time to look further. Irwin didn't know the name of the Kirov home agency but did some Googling. It was the Mega Agency with an address on SE Powell. Irwin didn't know where Powell was, but Google World did, and there it was: the street view of an single story brick office building, the picture taken when a gold BMW was parked in front. Had that been Kirov's car? There was no telling how old the picture was.

The Mega Agency had a web site that offered services, but also had a solicitation for potential home helpers. Complete discretion guaranteed. Did that mean they hired people who had something to hide?

Irwin Googled again. If your name shows up anywhere in the world, the search engine can find it. In this case, his search of the Mega Agency led to another murder, this time a poisoning of a resident of the Rose plaza by a girl using a stolen identity and employed by the Mega Agency.

Two murders at the Rose Plaza! Sounded like a crime-ridden placed for elderly tenants. No wonder that old lady had a gun even if it was a World War II souvenir.

Did Putinsky know the story of the murders?

If one of the Mega employees had used a stolen identity, were there others?

The rent-a-cop business was an entree to a lot of information, like surveillance equipment, burglar alarms, details burglars might find useful. It was not just for watching out for shoplifters. If Kirov had employed other girls with dubious back grounds, did he supply local brothels with fresh meat, runaway girls off the greyhound and ripe for plucking?

Irwin was beginning to see Portland as a very shady, even dangerous place. He hoped he didn't have to be like

Katja and carry a concealed hand gun. He had read comic reports of men who shot themselves in the foot or worse. If a man carried a loaded pistol in his pants pocket and scratched himself, there was as risk of being half cocked.

Maybe he should ask Katja about her romance with that Glock. .

CHAPTER EIGHTEEN

At Portland State University the new term was about to begin. It was already late for Irwin to look for a job interview at Portland State. He had sent his resume by email, but showed up hopefully at the foreign language department. A clerk who looked like a student wasn't friendly. A casual gesture showed there was a stack of other applications. The message was, "don't call us, we'll call you in case there's a cancellation." Russian was no longer in style. Better if he could teach Mandarin. Considering the insecurity of adjunct teaching jobs, even greeters at Wal-Mart had benefits How far did university administrators think the prestige of being a college teacher compensated for lack of job security?

Katja was on duty during orientation. The student union, Smith Hall, was crowded. It was an international student body with many Asians, girls with head scarves, much more multi-racial than Irwin had seen in the Upper Peninsula which was 99 percent white and, locally, Apostolic Lutheran.

In the park there was a noisy demonstration against campus police being armed. A man who tried to break up a fight had been shot dead by two campus cops. They'd been fired, but out on the mall Katja attracted attention. Campus cops, especially armed ones, had become the enemy.

Katja was followed back to the Avalon Arms and came to the front entrance in an agitated state. Irwin saw her on the front door monitor as she let herself into the building. He called out, "Katja, what's going on?"

He let her into the apartment.

Katja was flustered. Normally Katja was cool headed, but she must have been heckled. It was not smart to heckle an armed person. "They do not like that I have gun."

"But you have a carry permit."

"I do but not as campus security."

Irwin could not imagine her without her firearm. It was second nature for her to have that Glock. Irwin had never handled fire arms, had never hunted. He had grown up in South Bend, Indiana, not on a farm where everyone had at least a .22 rifle from childhood. To him, walking around with a hand gun was weird. Maybe that fit in in Portland which prided itself on being weird. If one wanted to be weird weren't tattoos and body piercing enough? "Why do you need it?"

She took off her bullet proof vest, dropped it on the floor and accepted a cup of coffee. "Vladimir say I should always have it for protection."

"Protection from what?" In the UP of Michigan there were bears, but they seldom came into town. The bears were the ones that needed protection from zealous home owners. Maybe people were overly protective of their garbage cans and, in spring, bird feeders.

Katja brushed a stray lock of her hair out of her eyes, sighed, sipped her coffee.

Irwin and Ivy sensed Katja was finally going to tell part of her story. She began, "In Moscow I was young Komsomol, like in USA Girl Scouts, but in Russia political. In school no religion classes like in USA Catholic schools, in Russia Marxism-Leninism."

Irwin remembered a locket he had seen in the Moscow GUM department store. It said "Lenin has lived, Lenin is living, Lenin shall live." Substitute for Jesus Christ. "So you were indoctrinated."

"They called it education. Vladimir said it was bullshit, but he would not say to anyone else, not even my mother."

"He didn't trust even his own wife?"

"In Russia you trust no one."

How well Irwin knew. Distrust was infectious. He had been betrayed by everyone, even his boss at the embassy. "But Vladimir trusted you."

"Vladimir had plans for me."

What were those plans? Irwin could guess but he wasn't ready to risk mentioning the term 'sleeper agent.' "Why do you always call him Vladimir?"

"Sometimes Vladi, when he is nice. He is not often nice."

"But not father?"

She shook her head and turned on her warmest smile. She had inherited the smile that had seduced him in Moscow. "You are my American papa."

That was gratifying. She knew how to melt his heart. Was it instinctive, or training in deception? "Security?" Irwin remembered the certificate Agent Burke had shown him. "That why he had you trained in marksmanship?"

"And other things."

"Like what?"

Now her eyes veiled. They had approached a red line. "Spy school." No further comment.

Maybe Agent Burke was right. Irwin waited for a clarification. All he got was Katja's shrug. "You understand, Vladimir is, was, KGB. If he was fisherman he would teach me how to catch fish. Is only natural."

Katja didn't want to say any more. She picked up her bulletproof vest and excused herself. She went up to her apartment to change clothes.

"So what do you think?" Ivy asked as she rinsed Katja's cup.

"About what?"

"You going to tell that Agent Burke that his suspicions are correct? That's she's a sleeper spy?"

"Just because she says she went to spy school doesn't make her a spy."

Ivy shook her head in disbelief. "Irwin, you're going down that path you got trapped in in Houghton. You cooperated with Agent Wilson in Marquette, reporting on those Moslem students. Now it looks to me like you're going to report on Katja. You're just as bad as the rest of them."

Irwin was defensive and indignant. "I'm not going to report on my daughter."

Ivy scoffed at him. "When the FBI comes to arrest her, are you going to stand by and watch?"

He had to admit to himself that he didn't know.

Ivy shook her head. "You know, in World War II in France the Underground would call you a collaborator. If you were a woman they'd shave your head."

Irwin wasn't familiar with World War II. That was long ago, before his time. "What did they do with men?"

"Sometimes they were hanged. The Vichy government was exiled."

"If they come for Katja we'll hide her."

"Oh?" Ivy was skeptical. "Irwin, you're chickenshit. That's why I was ready to divorce you when we left Michigan."

"I thought I was doing my duty against terrorism."

"So what are you going to tell that FBI agent Burke?"

"Nothing. He's mostly interested in Vladimir. Vladimir is not my friend."

"He's your boss, Irwin. He's our landlord. The two of you share a daughter."

Irwin sighed. "Where does that leave me?"

Ivy taunted him. "You are a co-conspirator, a fellow traveler. Agent Burke will see you as a traitor protecting a

Russian spy. When they come for Katja they'll sweep you up along with all the other dirt they can find."

"What about you?"

"Me? I'm going to protect my baby Isaac. I will not be separated from my kid like some illegal immigrant. If you get arrested I might visit you in jail Maybe once or twice a year. How about that?"

"Christ, Ivy. Don't do this. You're jumping to conclusions." But he knew the possibilities were real. "I've got to see Vladimir. He has an office at Lloyd's Center Mall where he has the security contract. If he's strictly legitimate, there's nothing to worry about."

"And if he's not?"

"We'll see."

Vladimir had taught Katja to trust no one. Was Irwin worthy of her trust? Trust was a fragile thing. Once broken, it would never be regained. He had been betrayed before. Being betrayed was terrible. He did not want to betray Katja.

CHAPTER NINETEEN

Irwin had never been to the Lloyd's Center shopping mall, at one time the largest in the United States. Originally open to the sky and the winter rains, it had been remodeled several times with the addition of a glass roof. Taking public transportation from the Avalon Arms was easy: the Portland street car had two loops, clockwise and counter clockwise. Both passed within a block or two of the mall. Irwin, by mistake, took the counterclockwise, which was the longest It crossed the Willamette River on the new suspension bridge but eventually got him close to his destination.

Katja told him Vladimir's office was on the third floor of the mall, the two lower levels occupied by shops. There was a food court and an ice skating rink where hopeful future Olympiads could train.

Vladimir's headquarters marked "Security" was at the end of a hard to find hallway, past the public toilets and a dentist's office. True to form, it had a surveillance camera mounted in the ceiling of the hallway, probably most useful in spotting people who sneaked shoplifted merchandise into the bath rooms.

Irwin let himself in. It looked like the office was also used as a break room for security staff. There was a coffee maker on a sideboard. A bored African-American uniformed rent-a-cop was idly reading the sports section of the Oregonian. Irwin approached the receptionist he had spoken with on the phone. "I'm Irwin Glass. Is Vladimir in?"

The receptionist was about thirty, blonde, with long hair down to her shoulders. One of his American students at Michigan Tech had said the women who worked at Ford wore short hair if they were married, long hair if they were in the market for a husband. Maybe there was something to the Moslem practice of hiding women's hair, something Orthodox Jews did, too, only with Jews it might be a wig, not a head scarf. An American girl with very short hair might be butch. Katja's hair was short. Did that mean something?

Putinsky's receptionist had been knitting at her desk, a ball of wool in an open drawer. She took one look at Irwin, sized him up as not a contender, and nodded him into Putinsky's office.

Putinsky got up from his chair and went around the desk to give Irwin a warm greeting, "Irvin!" like they were long lost buddies. The Russian hug and air kisses made him uncomfortable. His family weren't huggers. At the Hartshornes' in Ocala you were lucky to get a handshake.

"How do like your new digs?"

Digs? Had Vladimir been watching British movies? Or had he, in his eagerness to adopt his new country, mixed up idioms?

Irwin switched to Russian. "It's very nice. A lot better than Moscow." In Moscow his government assigned rooms had been in an old Soviet prefab made of standard concrete panels that leaked at the seams. He'd been afraid to open the window for fear the glass would fall out and into the street.

Putinsky's gesture was magnanimous "This is America."

"Not every place is like your apartment at the Mirabella."

"It is only money." Putinsky's grin told a lot. Not that he had earned it himself, but he had got away with it as long as his victims never caught up with him wanting it back.

"You also have the home helper service."

"You want a job? I do not think you want to baby sit elderly, infirm, handicapped old people."

"No. I read about the murder at the Rose Plaza."

Vladimir looked like he thought the comment was an accusation. "That was before my time."

"No, that was the Kirov brothers."

"The one that was killed."

"You did your home work"

Irwin gave a modest shrug. "How many work at the agency?"

Putinsky thought a moment. "About twenty. Home helper is not a good career. There is much turnover. Some of the girls go on to nursing school .Others like the flexible hours. The best are Russian women."

That recalled the sight of stout, babushka-clad women stoically sweeping the Moscow streets. "And here at the mall?"

"∶Have a dozen, but there are other places that need a guard, synagogues, the Jewish community center. The guards at the synagogues are armed. Here in the mall they are not."

"I suppose you don't want a shoot-out in a crowd of shoppers."

Vladimir had done his homework, too. "It happened in Clackamas Town Center. Fortunately, the shooter killed himself."

"If a security guard can't be armed, what's the use?"

Putinsky agreed. "We cannot use mace. If we lock a shop door to hold a shoplifter, it's kidnapping."

So what use were security guards? Irwin supposed they had to rely on cameras to collect evidence and even if identified and arrested, the jails were too full for such petty crimes.

Irwin wondered if Adat Israel in Michigan had had a guard would that fire bombing ever have happened, with Katja running after the kid and shooting him?

"I need to go over my duties as your building manager. If someone moves out, who handles the new rentals?"

"A real estate rental agency. No problem for you."

"I was going over the lease agreements. Is there something more I should know?"

Vladimir sat back down at his desk and swiveled in the executive chair. "We have two Russian couples, no children, on the top floor. They are looking to buy a house. I do not think they will stay long." He explained, "I like to keep those apartments for new immigrants."

It reminded Irwin of the chain migration Pakistanis used for the motel business. There was a network of people from the same family. In the early days before the immigration laws were tightened there were home town associations, people who banded together to assists members in bringing their families over. The Russians must have a similar arrangement. "Then it's good that I speak Russian."

Putinsky disagreed. "Russians have good English."

Irwin wondered if there was a pipeline for Russian immigrants. How would a hostile Russian government get its people into the United States? Student visas? Dissidents seeking political asylum like Vladimir? Not every would-be immigrant could claim an American college professor was her father. Of course, Vladimir wasn't a dissident. He was a fugitive from the cleptocracy and one of them himself. Only his KGB background made him a person of interest for a serious debriefing and resettlement.

"Are your old enemies still after you?"

The topic made Vladimir uncomfortable. "Most are dead. I was never political."

That was the difference. It was possible for a Russian oligarch to escape the country and avoid confiscation. To be a dissident meant jail or worse. That reminded Irwin of the turncoat who had been poisoned in England and barely survived. That was politics. Just being a crook didn't matter. Maybe Vladimir was safe.

Irwin hoped he and Ivy were. He didn't want a repeat of the home invasion in Houghton. The apartment he and Ivy shared did not have an emergency exit, not even onto a balcony like Katja's on the top floor. The bullet proof glass on the concierge's window had freaked him out. With all the security stuff, was Avalon Arms supposed to be a fortress? Not with ground floor windows out to the miniscule front yard, even if they didn't open.

Vladimir might claim he was safe. If so, why the armored Cadillac? Was it just old habits or genuine fear?

Putinsky asked, "How did you get here today?"

"Streetcar."

Putinsky slapped the side of his head. "Oh! I am sorry. I am forgetting in my old age. I will issue you a company car. It will say on it 'Security.' The company will cover the insurance. With such a car you might even be able to park free." He got up and went to a cupboard mounted on the back wall of the office, took down a set of car keys. "Our cars are parked on the upper deck."

Irwin took the set he was handed. The pair of keys were electronic, not like his old Toyota pickup. "How will I know which car?"

Putinsky laughed. "Just push the red button. The car will announce itself."

Irwin was bemused when he left the office. The mall was big, with several parking lots. He found the upper deck and saw a row of four security vehicle all lined up. He clicked the red button until he heard a persistent honking, saw headlights flash.

Putinsky's fleet of black security cars with a yellow stripe looked like they were all recycled, repainted Crown Victoria police vehicles once a favorite for law enforcement. They were equipped with rhino bars and probably with souped up engines. Recycled patrol cars were like hearses, seldom driven at highway speeds, except hearses were low mileage. These were certainly not new, the upholstery worn, the driver's seat sat out, and the rear seat smelling of something that had been nasty but had been cleaned up, more or less. What had that been? Blood? Vomit?

It had been easy to Find Lloyd's Center on the streetcar. Now that Irwin had to drive himself in Portland's maze of one way streets and crush of traffic, he was confused. He didn't have a map, just a general sense of direction. He didn't know how to work the on board GPS. But what the hell? Now he and Ivy had a free car. Coming from Vladimir Putinsky, he knew that nothing was free. Putinsky knew how to make a person beholden.

To get back to the Avalon Arms, Irwin remembered the streetcar had lead him from the Park Blocks to the mall, so he retraced its route to where he got off the street car and followed the tracks. It was not the quickest route, but he got to the apartment building, then realized he needed a garage door opener to get in. He used his basic track phone to call Ivy.

"Meet me at the garage. Vladimir has loaned us a car, but I don't have the door opener."

Standing in the open doorway, Ivy was impressed. "Katja will love this. With her campus cop uniform she can park anywhere."

Irwin found a supply of garage door openers in the concierge's office. The thought of Katja tooling around Portland in uniform in a recycled police car gave him second thoughts about her maturity. She was not a real cop. Except for her sidearm, she had no more authority than one of Putinsky's just for show mall guards. It was ludicrous, except she had killed two people.

What bothered him about those deaths was she didn't seem to care. When he cleaned up the blood in their kitchen floor in Houghton, he had been sick, in a state of shock. He couldn't forget the look on the home invader's face. He had been dead before he could be surprised. The dead eyes imprinted on Irwin's memory and would not got away.

Irwin had not served in the military, had never been to war, killed no one. He realized he had his own version of PTSD. Maybe not everyone did. Was Katja immune? Did she lack empathy? Like a well-trained killer, she had not hesitated to shoot, no remorse.

In a life or death situation you do not ponder or hesitate. You shoot. She did.

He had watched her cleaning her Glock. There was no hesitation as in "which part goes where?" She had practice. Was that what she learned in sharpshooter class in Russia?

It was in sharp contrast to the Katja who had rinsed our her underwear in their Houghton bath room sink and hung it over the bath tub without any embarrassment. Ivy had noticed it, too. Maybe in Communist Russia in crowded, communal quarters at a boarding school one became accustomed. Katja was not shy.

Katja had not grown up in Irwin's household. She had simply arrived, whole, without a shared past. For all their family togetherness, he had to admit he hardly knew her. She was his daughter, but she was a stranger, a stranger with a gun.

CHAPTER TWENTY

Though Irwin now had a security vehicle that looked like police but wasn't, he didn't feel like testing the system of parking violations in Portland. The city had given up on the old fashioned parking meters that worked with coins and opted for solar powered permit dispensers. To discourage city parking, it could cost four dollars to park in a two hour zone. For what little business Irwin had with the FBI, he could phone.

After his first meeting with Agent Burke he was known to the gate keeper receptionist and put though. After the preliminaries, he got to his question. "Agent Burke, just what is a so-called sleeper agent? Is it like that old movie 'The Manchurian Candidate" where a post hypnotic signal turns the agent into an assassin?"

Agent Burke was apparently not a fan of old movies on the Turner Classic channel. "Not exactly. A sleeper agent blends into the society and is only activated when needed. Such people might hide in plain sight for years."

"And you think my daughter Katja is a sleeper agent?" Irwin insisted on re-enforcing his claim that Katja was his daughter no matter how much the FBI suspected she was a plant.

"That's the theory."

So Burke wasn't so sure. "So what's she supposed to do? Hijack a plane and fly into the World Trade Center?? On demand? What? With a phone call that gives the password that sets her off?"

"We don't know."

"And on the strength of that suspicion, that guess, your agency was willing to help fund our move from Florida to Portland?"

"That's our cover story."

"Oh, so there's something else.?" There had to be an ulterior motive.

"Vladimir Putinsky."

That made more sense. Irwin launched into his oral report. "I saw Vladimir at his office at the Lloyd Center mall. Looks legitimate to me. He also bought the franchise for a home helper agency. Oh, and a luxury apartment at the Mirabella." He didn't mention the armored Cadillac SUV or where the money for all this had come from.

"He made you the manager of his apartment building, the Avalon Arms, right?"

"Yes. Since I hadn't found a job in Florida and Ivy would only be part time at the college there, it was a good deal for us."

"He knows you from his interrogation in Virginia. I've seen the file. That got him asylum in this country, but he really doesn't owe you anything, Mr. Glass. What do you think is his real motivation?"

"Maybe it's family," Irwin suggested. "Vladimir and I are co-fathers to Katja."

Burke wasn't convinced. "I saw the transcripts. When you turned down his pitch to work for the KGB didn't he threaten to kill you?"

Irwin had forgotten that bad moment in Gorki Park. Suppressed memory?

While he thought about that one, Burke had another line of argument. "Vladimir Putinsky will want a pay back.

That sort of man doesn't do anything out of the goodness of his heart. He wants something from you."

"So do you." Who was Irwin being the foil for? Were both those forces playing him for some hidden motive? Katja knew he had talked with the FBI when they visited in Ocala. He also had a history, not a very good one, with Vladimir from those days in Moscow that ruined his State Department career. By rights, Irwin should hate the man. That was a long time ago. Now Vladimir was trying to make a new life in America. Irwin was not a hater. Like they say, time heals all wounds.

Something didn't make sense. He was sure Katja was at the center of it, whether she was some sort of sleeper or not.

"See what your bloodhound instincts can sniff out, Mr. Glass. Keep in touch."

End of conversation.

Vladimir Putinsky was an enigma. So was Katja.

Why couldn't life be simple? Just keep his marriage together and enjoy little Isaac? The kid was sitting up now, discovering the world. There was still something called innocence. There was joy in that.

Ivy had not been part of the conversation with Agent Burke. "What did he say?"

"He says Vladimir has an ulterior motive."

"For playing the part of benefactor?"

"I'm not so sure about being a benefactee." Irwin was a bit overwhelmed by the job of building manager. He had never had that kind of responsibility. "My job isn't one of those straw positions where you never show up and get paid. This isn't Chicago."

Home is where you hang your hat. Ivy was a person who could make herself at home anywhere. She had adapted to life in a Lanai in Florida. The apartment in Portland was a big step up. She didn't have to worry about the rent or the utilities. They even had the use of a car, if you didn't mind looking like you stole a police vehicle.

Motivation, motivation. Because of bad experience, Irwin was instinctively suspicious. His imagination went wild. What about the two Russian couples on the fourth floor? Were they legitimate? Or was Vladimir importing sleeper agents in spite of being "retired" from the KGB or whatever they called in nowadays? Maybe using Katja as a ticket to US immigration Vladimir could be a sponsor for a stream of secret agents. Vladimir had apparently unlimited sources of cash. Was this all his stolen stash? Or was he bankrolled by the Russian cleptocracy?

To do what? Rig American elections? Steal technology? Was Irwin an unwitting part of a vast conspiracy? Was Vladimir one of those plants like a poplar tree to send out under ground roots in all directions to create a forest?

Paranoia was one disease. Conspiracy theories were another. Let this speculation get out of control and you could go nuts.

Finally unable to stand it any longer, Irwin called Vladimir.

How should he put it? "Vladimir," he began in Russian to give the impression that they were on intimate terms. "I appreciate your fixing me up with a job and an apartment for me and my family, but you didn't have to do that. Did you have some special reason?"

Vladimir hesitated. He started to speak a couple of times, finally admitted, "I have not been a good father to Katja. As her American papa as she calls you, living in the same building you can give her moral support. She is, I'm afraid, sometimes unstable. She trusts you, Irvin. I want you to keep your eyes on her."

"Oh?"

"It is no more than any father would do for his daughter."

"I see."

"Katja is like a tiger. She is unpredictable. She needs what a sailor would call a steady hand at the helm."

Unpredictable? Like what? Who she might shoot next time? Irwin reluctantly had to agree. In the past Katja had disappeared without warning and never explained her absence. He didn't feel he had any ability to steer her in any direction.

Ivy might. It could be a woman to woman thing.

Katja had lost her mother and Vladimir had been at best absentee. Ivy could be a good influence, especially in areas that intimidated Irwin. For instance, was Katja a virgin? That was something Irwin was embarrassed to talk about with his would be daughter.

Irwin ended the conversation with thanks and a promise to do what he could.

Now not only the FBI wanted him to watch Katja, but so did Vladimir.

Why couldn't life be simple and domestic? Like giving Isaac his first solid food? Dogs knew the world through their noses, humans with their mouths. The look on Isaac's face when Ivy tried to give his a spoonful of Gerber spinach was funny. What a face the kid made!

As for Katja, what was his next move?

TWENTY-ONE

It was one of the last hot days of Portland's summer. Irwin saw Katja coming across the Park Blocks in her campus cop uniform. She let herself into the building. As she passed the concierge's window she tapped the bulletproof glass and waved. She was perspiring, didn't stop to say hello but strode for the elevator.

"I'll bet Katja will be excited to know Vladimir has loaned us a car," Irwin said. "I'll take her one of the keys."

"Tell her not to go joy riding around town. It is sort of an official car."

Irwin took the elevator up to the fourth floor, knocked at Katja's door. He heard her say something, then, using his manager's pass key, let himself in.

Except that it had only one bedroom, the apartment was almost identical to his own. The first thing he saw was the campus cop uniform hung over one of the tall stools at the bar, the holstered Glock on the seat. Then he saw Katja.

"I'm taking a shower," she explained.

She was naked, made no attempt to hide herself.

Was she flaunting her body at him? Ivy was a modest person. Even though they were married he seldom saw his wife totally naked. When they had sex she wanted the light out. In the chill of Houghton's seven month winter, she preferred for them to be under a sheet or a blanket.

Katja was different. Standing nude in front of the man she called her American papa didn't faze her a bit.

Irwin didn't have to dwell on the sight or stare. It was one of those images that imprinted like forever on his memory and blended with another image, that of Svetlana, her mother, in the bedroom of the Metropole hotel. Ivy's breasts were normally average, maybe a B cup if Irwin knew the sizes of women's underwear, but of course now that she was nursing her breasts were enlarged. Katja's mother's breasts were not perky like some teen-ager's but they were still youthful. Eventually all breasts sag, thanks to gravity. Katja's were larger than Ivy's and worthy of some porn star without the enhancement of silicone.

Svetlana's public hair had been a dark bush. Katja was shaved.

She gave him a wanton smile. "You staring at me, papa?"

He was embarrassed. "You have a scar on your chest under your, er, left breast."

She touched the scar as if remembering. "An accident."

"Accident?"

She reconsidered. "Training accident. We were doing martial arts. Self defense."

"With knives?" The very thought gave Irwin the creeps.

"For realism."

Irwin shook his head. This must have been something in the spy school she had mentioned.

Katja had almost put on a white terrycloth bath robe. She slipped it on now. "When you do martial arts, you must never lose your temper."

Irwin knew nothing of martial arts, but he had heard that professional wrestling matches were just for show unless one of the fighters got mad. That's when real injuries happened. "So did you lose your temper?"

Katja was apologetic. "He did. And I was careless because he was angry, so he cut me."

"What did you do then?"

"A reflex. Broke his arm. Head lock. I killed him." It was said off hand, without inflection, as if killing someone meant no more than having a beer.

"What, like in the movie 'Kill Bill'"?

She had seen the film. In the end Bill is grasped in some secret combination of Oriental pressure points that paralyzes him in a set of spasms and he dies.

"No. That takes too long." She approached him and held out her hands. "I could kill you in two seconds."

Irwin stepped back. He knew she could and was afraid. He gasped. "I hope you never get angry with me."

Katja shook her head. "Why would I? I love you. You are my papa."

He knew that love was an emotion that could quickly flip. He had seen how Ivy could be affectionate and tender, then be set off by some wrong statement and be icy cold. That's what happens in lover's quarrels. After sex she asks "how was it for you?" There is no safe answer. Even "great" may be interpreted as insincere and a lie.

Irwin swallowed. "I love you, too, Katja. I am grateful that you are my daughter." Was he begging for his life? He was grateful that she was not his enemy. His natural instinct was to be afraid of her.

Vladimir must know about the martial arts incident. No wonder he was concerned.

Katja opened the bathrobe to show him the goods. "Do I remind you of my mother?"

When she looked at him like that, she did. "Sometimes." He could not help but compare the image of the mother with the daughter. Both burned like snapshots in his memory. When a men's blood rushes to his penis his brain shuts off. Of course, in Moscow there had been no conversation about anything. Svetlana had handed him a glass of vodka. He drank. Beyond that he remembered nothing but how she looked naked and later came to out on the street.. Now it was Katja in all her youthful, sexy glory.

"You want to have sex with me?"

How much she was like her mother. He was a man,. after all, susceptible to invitation. That's what got him into all that trouble in Moscow. His brain was shutting off. Irwin stammered. "We don't do incest in our family."

She laughed. "Maybe another time."

Irwin took a deep breath and tried to focus. "The reason I came up was to give you a key to our car. Vladimir has loaned us one of his security vehicles. It's a recycled police car, so don't break any speed limits. It's down in the garage."

He put the key down on the galley counter and fled.

Downstairs. Back in their apartment he told Ivy what happened. It all came out in a confused muddle. "She was naked. Wanted to have sex with me."

Ivy had suggested it before. She'd easily noticed how he looked at Katja. Ivy said if Katja wasn't his real daughter, and they got a divorce he could take on Katja even if she was twenty years or so younger. "So did you?"

"No." Next she would ask him if he wanted to. He didn't want to go there. Instead, he said, "I want to have sex with you."

She glanced at his tight pants. "I see you are inspired. Lucky us."

The screened in Lanai in Ocala at the Hartshornes' had not been a private place. Portland was different. This was the best sex they'd had in months.

In the midst of their sex Ivy asked, "So are you imagining sex with me or with Katja?"

It was another of those fatal questions. Not even "no comment" would do. "I'm with you." It was an evasion, but she pretended it was satisfactory..

In the afterglow, nuzzling Ivy's neck he asked, "Has she ever hit on you?"

"No, why?"

"She struck me as someone with, well, strong appetites."

Ivy rolled over and looked him in the eye. "You're thinking of a threesome, right?"

"I didn't say that."

"I know you, Irwin. You wouldn't cheat on me but if we were three you'd join in."

"Well… I never thought about it."

"But you're thinking about it now."

"You're putting ideas in my head." After a hesitation he added, just to tease. "Sounds like fun."

She gave him a throaty, wanton laugh and snuggled closer. "You up for another round?"

When she put it that way, he was.

She surprised him afterwards when they were cleaning up. As she was wiping herself with a towel she saw him staring. "You saw Katja naked."

"Yes."

"Was she shaved down here?"

"Yes."

"You think I should shave my pussy?"

"Might avoid me getting hair in my teeth."

She rolled her eyes. "Sounds like a reason."

"You want me to shave you?" It seemed to Irvin a delicate operation. He sometimes nicked his chin while shaving.

"Maybe Katja could shave me." She hesitated. "And no, you don't get to watch."

"Shucks."

CHAPTER TWENTY-TWO

How could he report this to Agent Burke? Certainly not the naked confrontation. Irwin didn't wan to describe his Russian daughter as some sort of a nymphomaniac or like Svetlana, her mother, who had been coerced by Vladimir into pretending to have sex with his blackmail victims. Instead, when he phoned, he simply reported, "Katja told me she killed her martial arts instructor back in Moscow."

Burke was interested. "How's that?"

"They were practicing self defense. He had a knife and cut her. She broke his arm and killed him with a head lock. She even offered to demonstrate for me."

"Did she?"

"If she did, I'd be dead."

"You want to write up that report?"

"Never. I don't do written reports. Not anymore. You never know who reads those or how they can be misinterpreted." He didn't want a repeat of what happened in Michigan.

Burke would have been happier if he had a file-able document, not just a conversation over the phone. "You satisfied with how I tell it?"

"I don't know how you'll report this or to whom. What's important, so far as I see it, isn't that she killed him. She knows how. It was a training accident. What gets me is she has no remorse."

"You think she's a sociopath?"

"That would make her a good CEO or even a president, charming but ruthless."

"All the more reason to keep tabs on her."

There was more to it than that. "Her Russian father, Vladimir Putinsky, seems to think the same thing. He sent her to spy school in Moscow."

"And you still think she's just your sweet, pretty Russian daughter."

After the naked confrontation he wasn't so sure about sweet. "A pretty Russian daughter who happens to carry a gun."

Agent Burke cleared his throat. "If I were you, Mr. Glass, I'd sleep with one eye open."

The Glasses still hadn't fully settled in Portland. Besides not yet familiar with the other tenants of the Avalon Arms, Irwin remembered that they didn't have health insurance. Though he and Ivy were healthy, they had little Isaac to worry about. He would need a doctor, immunization shots, and a regular checkup. Then there was Katja. Under the Affordable Care Act a college student could stay on her parent's insurance until she was twenty-six years old. Did his made up job for Putinsky include benefits?

Life was full of details, like now he would need an Oregon driver's license. He'd avoided getting one in Florida, but now they had apparently made a permanent move.

Then there were other mundane things, like groceries and replenishing their supply of disposable diapers. At least now they had a car to transport bulky purchases. It would be nice to have a folding stroller so Isaac wouldn't have to be carried. He was growing fast. Must be that mother's milk.

A call to Putinsky's office at the Lloyds Center mall was fruitful. Yes, there were benefits to working for Vladimir. He would send over the health insurance papers to sign.

After nursing Isaac Ivy helped him work up a grocery list. He headed for the garage and the company car. Safeway was only a few blocks away on Jefferson street.

When he got back with several bags he let himself into the apartment. He unpacked, put the cold stuff in the fridge and crept toward the nursery with the diapers, not wanting to wake up Isaac if he was asleep. As he passed their closed bedroom door he heard laughter.

Then the laughter turned to giggles, then moans. What the hell?

He looked in.

Ivy had not waited to follow through on their conversation about pussy shaving. There she was in their bed with Katja. One thing had led to another.

Irwin had never witnessed lesbian love.

He didn't know what to say, maybe best nothing, maybe just walk away and close the door but then another surprise. Ivy saw him hesitate uncertainly in the doorway, teased him with an invitation. "Care to join us?"

He realized she was testing him to see if he'd refuse. If he did, there might not be another chance, now that Katja had aroused his curiosity and lust. He didn't answer, just started taking off his clothes. "Is this a lesson in martial arts?"

Ivy had a spelling suggestion. "Maybe marital arts.".

Katja didn't say anything. Her face was buried between Ivy's thighs. Apparently the shaving session was a success.

This was something else Irwin was not going to report to agent Burke. Definitely not.

A new chapter in the Katja story had begun.

CHAPTER TWENTY-THREE

An odd, totally unexpected transformation had taken place. Ivy had always been shy, inhibited, didn't show herself to him naked even though they were married. Now, with Katja, it was a party. The three of them stood in the large shower stall for back scrubs with giggles and laughter.

Irwin was confused. The sudden transition had him wondering about Ivy, about his relationship with Katja. If she wasn't really his daughter, as the FBI asserted, having threesome sex wasn't such an immoral act, but he did not want to get Katja pregnant.

He could not see himself accepting Katja's invitation for sex if it was clear adultery. He had to draw the line someplace. Though he had thought Ivy was inhibited, he was, too, conventional to a fault. But nothing about his life since Moscow had been conventional.

In Moscow he had rejected the option of becoming a double agent, lost his security clearance and his job. It was all because of Vladimir Putinsky. Having forfeited all hope for a foreign service career, he had tried to rebuild his own persona as a college instructor. Then Katja had shown up, a blast from the past as it were, a blast he was ashamed of for being duped by Svetlana and Vladimir. He had no memory of what happened after that drink of vodka. He had seen the sex photos Putinsky had shown him in the Astoria restaurant when he made his pitch but he didn't remember it. Yet here she was, his alleged daughter, looking so much like his brief recollection of her mother, wanting sex. Like Reagan had said, here we go again.

The FBI only made things more complicated, that conflict between being a good citizen against terrorism and a duplicitous faculty advisor to the Moslem Students Association, with terrible result. Another job lost.

Again he would have to rebuild his life. Being a husband and father of baby Isaac was a stable platform he could happily live with, except now it came with ironic conditions, like working for his old nemesis Vladimir Putinsky, and conspiring, yes it was conspiring, with the FBI. Actually being a building manager for Vladimir Putinsky, even if he was no longer KGB, made it look like the controlling Putinsky had finally won. Irwin was unfinished business, Putinsky's lackey.

Now this new development, uninhibited threesome sex with Katja. Was that part of Putinsky's plan?

Irwin rationalized that Vladimir was no longer KGB. He was a businessman in Portland, Oregon, even if he did it with stolen Russian Mafia money. Though Irwin had refused the option once offered by embassy security to work with them as a double agent, now he was working, sort of, with the FBI and the old enemy was, maybe the same.

Irwin was bewildered. Then there was Katja. It might be possible to pretend the three way sex didn't happen, that it was a fluke, a one off event. Everyone would put their clothes back on and resume their comfortable, conventional roles. Except they didn't.

Ivy and Katja were like a couple of school girls playing double dare. I double dare you to go naked in front of Irwin. See if he blushes. See if he gets a hard on. Ivy, always proper, now suddenly was quite unabashed to walk around their apartment naked, and Katja was right along with her like a couple of nudists flaunting their bodies at him.

What was he expected to do? Cavort along with them? He was too inhibited.

Irwin rationalized that for Ivy nakedness had already been happening by stages. When you are nursing a baby, showing your otherwise modestly concealed breast becomes a nearly public spectacle. On a French or Danish beach going topless was no big deal, but Irwin had never been to France or Denmark. Nor had he been to a nudist camp where it was taboo to look at someone below the shoulders.

Irwin wasn't ready for that. He wasn't comfortable with the two women staring at his private parts to see if their antics got him going. The least inhibited he could be was to go about just in his Fruit of the Loom underpants, the same brand he'd been wearing when found drunk and arrested on the Moscow street. Whenever he saw the label he remembered.

Ivy had teased him about Katja, said she saw how he looked at her. He'd put it down to jealousy, the awkwardness about sharing the Houghton, Michigan house with a svelte Russian girl. It had been Ivy's space. She did not want competition as the alpha female and sensed that Katja might be a competitor.

Now the two women had turned into a lesbian couple. Was Irwin just an appendage? Just a guy in a woman's world? A pet cock?

It certainly felt that way when Ivy and Katja left him in the apartment as baby sitter for Isaac. He didn't like to shop, so the two women went off, like girl friends, not step mother and adopted daughter, looking for a baby stroller and whatever it was that women shopped for.

They were suddenly a threesome. It was not unheard of. A documentary film about the creator of Wonder Woman told of that family, one man, two women, and the four children it produced, each woman having two of the kids.

Was this going to be his story, too? He couldn't imagine it. He was too conventional.

And all this while Vladimir Putinsky, the FBI, and potentially Vladimir's old enemies hung over them like dark clouds threatening stormy weather.

When they came back from shopping he had Isaac in his car seat strapped to one of the bar stools while he entertained the kid. "Daddy's making supper for all of us. Would you like mashed potatoes? Can you say da-da?"

"Ma-ma." It was a start.

Isaac liked the stirring spoon. Once tasted, it made a nice noise when banged on the counter.

As soon as Ivy returned she explained, "I had to come back. My milk started and I knew Isaac was hungry. It's like remote control." She unceremoniously stripped again and offered Isaac her breast.

Irwin had made dinner for three, pork chops, mashed potatoes, and green beans. For Isaac he mashed some of the beans in the blender. Watching Isaac suckle he said, "I think he likes boob better than beans."

The real reason he made supper for three was he wanted to sound Katja out about Svetlana. It was a domestic scene, Irwin serving from the cook's side of the counter, Katja looking much at home. She was not wearing her usual lipstick. Sitting topless, showing off in only thong underwear, there was no place for her Glock. Obviously with Irwin and Ivy she felt safe. He liked that, for the gun always made him nervous.

Since they were a family on intimate terms, he'd take a chance. "Tell me about your mother."

Katja looked relaxed. After an afternoon of sex and a communal shower, all the barriers of intimidation were down. "I not see much of my mother. When I was about three Vladimir put me in communal day care. Later a boarding school, then spy school. He wanted me to be like him, a young Komsomol, a good Communist."

Ivy was curious. "Sounds like you were brainwashed."

Katja disagreed. "I rebelled. The few times they were together I see that Vladimir is cruel to my mother. "

"They didn't live together?"

"No. He said I was not his child. He took me away from Svetlana as punishment."

Irwin understood. "He's what we call a control freak."

Isaac was ready to be burped. Irwin handed Ivy a dish towel to put over her shoulder so if he spit up it wouldn't go down her back. She lifted him out of his car seat to take him into the nursery for a change of diaper.

Katja told another side of Svetlana's story. "Vladimir forced Svetlana to pose for honey pot pictures. For blackmail. She hated it. She deliberately got pregnant when she was with you, the American." Katja smiled slyly as if she'd secretly witnessed the act of her own conception.. Had Putinsky shown her the photographs? "She told me you were my American father. She said you were a nice guy."

"So I was her revenge."

"Then Vladimir took me away from her as punishment."

Irwin had no difficulty imagining Vladimir exerting his power as a KGB officer. Ruthlessness went with the territory. "So what were Svetlana's plans?"

Katja shook her head sadly. "Nothing. She got cancer. Only when she was dieing did she tell me her story."

"And then Vladimir sent you to America?"

Katja smiled coyly. She had finished her pork chop and turned her fork in the last of the potatoes. "To my American papa." The look she gave him spoke volumes. Intimate knowledge. Affection. Maybe amusement. Possessiveness. Love?

"Lucky us," Irwin said, leaning across the counter to kiss her, as fatherly as he dared, on the forehead. .

"That depend on Vladimir."

"What do you mean?"

Her look told him she was not yet free. "He has plans."

That could mean anything. Putting Irwin in the building manager's job, potentially a clearing house for embedded Russian spies was one possibility. Could Vladimir still bear a grudge because Irwin had refused to be ensnared in that honey pot scheme in Moscow? Some people have long memories. Some never forget. Grudges never die.

Always suspicious, Irwin wondered if their cozy little love nest might be part of Vladimir's aborted Moscow plan. Was Katja's role chapter two? Katja was as willing as Svetlana had been, or appeared to be, in that Metropole hotel room. He tried to shake off the thought. The threesome with Ivy had to have been spontaneous. Then again, did Svetlana tell her daughter that she had actually had sex with him because he "had a nice cock"? Would she tell her own daughter that? Did that make Katja curious?

With a shudder he realized doubt and suspicion could destroy him.

CHAPTER TWENY-FOUR

With Katja back in her apartment and Isaac tucked in his crib Irwin and Ivy settled down on the couch for some TV. The evening news was the usual mix of sound bites interspersed with commercials, ending with a feel good story so the public wouldn't sign off in a state of frustration and anxiety.

Together in that nice apartment life was good.

Irwin was worried about their expenses. They were building up credit card debt he didn't want. "The stroller looks nice. How much was it?"

Ivy cuddled him, her face against his chest. "Don't worry about it. Katja paid. She says it's her present."

"She must still be living off Vladimir's stolen money."

They didn't know.

"About this afternoon..." he began.

"That was fun."

"It was a surprise," he admitted. "I never thought you'd do..."

"Do what?"

"Lesbian stuff. She seduced you."

Ivy laughed. "And you joined in."

"Well…" Embarrassed, he evaded that topic. "I don't want to get Katja pregnant. Is she on the pill?"

Ivy looked at him, her eyes searching. "I'll ask her."

"When you're done nursing Isaac, I guess you'll be going back on it."

Ivy sighed. "It may be too late for that."

"What? You're not pregnant again? Already?"

"Not while I'm lactating. I'm afraid my biological clock has run its course. No more babies for me. No little sister for Isaac. Isaac was my only chance." She hugged him, a sad face.

"Mine, too." He had a feeling that they had passed an important turning point with no return. They had no siblings, both the only child in the household.

"Buck up. You're going to be a good Dad, Irwin."

There was a pause while they both ruminated. Finally Ivy said, "I think we should have some ground rules."

"About us?"

"About Katja. I don't want you up in her apartment having sex."

"What about down here?"

"Only if I'm with you."

"OK."

"And no impregnation, Irwin. If I think it's OK for you to fuck her I'll buy you some condoms.

Ivy didn't usually use such language. "So that'll be your signal? Hand me a condom?"

Another pause. Then she added. "Some French women don't mind if their husbands have a mistress. Takes some of the obligation out of their having boring sex."

Though it might be flattering to his manliness, Irwin didn't like the idea of what he saw was as being pet cock. What was the male equivalent of a mistress? Resident lover?

He knew that a one night stand was often just that. Once curiosity was satisfied there was no reason to continue. People had different expectations. Bam, bam, thank you ma'am. He was satisfied and she was disappointed. Therein lay the trap.

He didn't know whether their afternoon romp was a one off or not. He could see that if Ivy was not in the mood, she'd be glad to provide him with condoms for her own relief. He had no inkling of what Katja would say about it. She struck him as a woman with appetites that might be insatiable. Some bachelors with dreams of glory might view the situation as idyllic. When did sex become an obligation?

Sex at home was much more convenient than going out to look for it elsewhere, and safer.

He worried too much. That was his nature.

Then there was the risk in provoking a woman who had a gun and knew how to break your neck in two seconds. If fun turned to fight it could be like the mongoose and the cobra or the male spider about to be eaten once her purpose had been satisfied. Rough sex with Katja could be deadly. What could be exciting for some was sometimes fatal, not his idea of fun..

Most of the time what we expect doesn't happen, like getting all your wishes from Santa. Fortunately, that also applies to what we are afraid of. Best to let things happen without too much ruminating about it.

He turned to his task of building manager. With the stack of rental contracts on a clipboard, he took the elevator up to Katja's fourth floor and knocked at the door to 4B.

He knew the tenants were a couple of Russian immigrants, Igor and Natasha Kakievich, a name reminiscent of the famous novel Dead Souls.

Natasha Kakievich came to the door. She was about five foot five, with a round face and a figure that suggested too much pizza or, in her case, piroshka. She was not obese, but could easily lose twenty pounds. She had dead, bleached blonde hair and wore a loose house dress of a gaudy flower print.

When Irwin addressed her in Russian her face briefly lit up then lapsed into suspicion. Perhaps she remembered stories of KGB knocks at the door followed by disappearance.

"I'm Irwin Glass, the building manager. Vladimir Putinsky hired me."

She wanted to know his credentials. "You know Putinsky?"

"From Moscow days." He made it sound like they were old comrades, but that could mean anything. He added, "Katja in the front apartment is our daughter." He hoped that reference didn't confuse. It could be interpreted that he and Vladimir were a gay couple with an adopted daughter, one of those weird Portland combinations.

"Oh." She stepped back to let him into the apartment.

The mismatched furniture looked like it had been rented, an inexpensive alternative to buying a suite of new, bargain furniture that soon wore out, no interest payments for sixty months no money down.

Natasha asked, "Are you Russian?"

"American. I once worked in Moscow."

"Ah." I was a comment that could mean anything or nothing. Thankfully, no follow-up question.

Irwin consulted his clipboard. "Your husband is Igor?"

"DA. He work at Intel. Computer engineer."

In the Communist Soviet Union everyone was an engineer as if titles compensated for low pay and no authority.

A Russian working at Intel might have the kind of access for industrial espionage Putinsky could be interested in. Agent Burke would be, too. Did the FBI watch everybody?

If everybody watched everybody there'd be full employment with nothing ever done.

"If you have any questions or need anything, let me know. My office is on the ground floor just inside the entrance. That's where you leave your rent check."

Rent. That was another of his responsibilities. If a tenant didn't pay did he hand the task over to Putinsky for eviction and all that nastiness? Something else to worry about. He had no idea how you could evict anyone or what their rights were.

She thanked him and he left.

He worked his way through the list. In all, sixteen units. The Saudi students were not in. One third floor apartment was in the name of Wong, two girls possibly sisters, also not at home.

He must have some business cards printed up, Irwin Glass, building manager.

It was a young crowd. Since there were no children in the building besides baby Isaac, it looked like a combination of students and young professionals, either still in school or not well off enough to buy their own condos if they ever did pay off their perpetual student loans. The rent was too expensive for the Avalon Arms to be full of noisy teen agers who threw all night parties. Because it was an apartment building there was no lobby, no communal space where people might congregate except for the laundry room adjacent to the basement garage. That was the only place residents were likely to run into each other.

Irwin inspected that, too. There were three washers and three driers, all coin operated. There was also, thankfully, a change machine or as concierge he might be perpetually pestered for quarters. Washers and driers were notorious for breaking down. What would he do then? Call Vladimir? There must be a maintenance contract.

In a utility closet he found, besides brooms and buckets, a menacing toilet plunger. Sixteen apartments, sixteen toilets. Foreign students might not know better than to flush un-flushable objects. He cringed at the thought of fishing out bloody menstrual nastiness.

The more Irwin thought about his duties the more he realized that the Avalon Arms was really like a big machine with many parts that needed maintenance. There was more to it than occasionally changing a light bulb in the hallway. He was not a landlord who lived abroad in Costa Rica and collected rents. He was going to be busy.

Over the next weeks Irwin's management chores settled into a routine. Summer ended. The Park Blocks were littered with fallen leaves. The rains came.

Isaac stood bouncing in his crib like a baby bird trying out its wings. He crawled, and looked about ready to walk. He was on solid food, had teeth. Ivy stopped nursing. It was beginning to look like a new, normal life, except with one notable exception: Katja.

CHAPTER TWENTY-FIVE

With the start of classes Katja's life settled into a routine. Besides her courses, she worked part time as a campus cop, wearing her uniform to classes, always armed in spite of some protests.

The reason for the protests was a couple of the other campus security guards had shot and killed an African-American who tried to break up a fight. It was a misunderstanding. The police were fired; the case still pending. All the security guards had to take twenty hours of training, particularly not to draw a weapon unless engaging an active shooter. There were allegedly non-lethal methods for subduing someone, but the fine print said a taser could occasionally cause a fatal heart attack, and people with respiratory problems could die from a pepper spray. Nothing was one hundred percent safe.

There were noisy demonstrations, students with signs and a bull horn asking that the campus police not be armed.

They had first been armed because a girl was raped on her way home one night. The South Park Blocks outside the entrance to the Avalon Arms were heavily wooded, like an urban forest, and lacked the otherwise well-placed CCT cameras. Katja was put on evening patrol, walking the campus and the park until eleven PM.

She was warned not to shoot anybody. Then, after being stalked for a couple of hours by a meth addict she was accosted. He pulled a knife. This time she was not cut and she did not kill him like she had her instructor in Russia. She simply crushed his windpipe with one blow and radioed for an ambulance to take him to the OHSU emergency room. With a crushed voice box he could no longer speak.

The story was prominent in the campus newspaper, The Vanguard.

After that, in addition to her regular workouts in the gym, she was in demand by the other security guards who wanted to learn martial arts. The trouble was, what she had been trained in that Moscow spy school was not to disable an attacker, but to kill him as quickly and soundlessly as possible It was the difference between sport self defense and the real thing.

Rumors move fast. After the windpipe story in the Vanguard, everyone knew she was deadly. Nobody bothered her. Nobody asked her for a date, either. Students were afraid of her. It wasn't just the uniform and the ever present Glock, which remained in its holster, but her reputation. She was shunned.

Katja fell back on her family for consolation. Suppers with Irwin and Ivy and playtime with Isaac were her comfort zone. This was home.

In Houghton, Michigan they had shared an entire house. In Portland they had separate apartments, but Katja used hers only to sleep and do her homework. They had returned to their cozy family relationship, and then some, all hanging out together.

There was hardly any need to get dressed. If Irwin was comfortable in his Fruit of the Loom tightie whities, that was OK as long as nobody came to the concierge's window and rang the bell. He'd put on a shirt before pulling up the privacy blind.

One evening, after cleaning up after supper, Katja asked, "Have you met the Russians on my floor?"

"Boris and Natasha Kakievich, yes. I met Natasha, but not Boris. He works at Intel, has a long commute on the Max."

Katja was suspicious. "Boris has a special work permit visa."

Ivy knew about that arrangement. "There's a shortage of American technical personnel."

"That's not what I mean. Boris knows Vladimir."

Irwin had suspected Putinsky was importing Russians as a sort of chain immigration. "Knows him personally?"

"*Njet*. By reputation. The Russian community all know he is a defector."

Irwin knew about rumors and the grapevine. They were why he'd lost his job at Michigan Institute of Technology. Too much gossip. "There are many ways to get into this country besides immigration under the quotas, like visitors' and student visas."

"My student visa would end if I weren't in school," Katja said. "But thanks to you, papa, I don't need a visa. I am an American now."

Being reminded of that suspect situation made Irwin uncomfortable. "So Boris knows Vladimir is a defector? Some people who are of special interest to the CIA and FBI come in as defectors in exchange for their information."

Ivy asked, "What does Boris think Vladimir is? A war criminal?"

"Is possible."

"A criminal, yes, but maybe just a thief, not someone who has done ethnic cleansing of Chechens."

Katja shook her head.

Katja had become a Blazer fan. Tonight she was wearing a black training bra and a pair of Blazer shorts. Many students were fans of the two warring Oregon colleges, so wore symbols of the Ducks or simply O. The soccer team was the Blazers. "Boris says Vladimir has enemies."

Ivy's nose wrinkled at the memory. "He hasn't heard of that home invasion in Houghton, I hope."

Katja had no idea.

Irwin asked, "You afraid someone is going to break in here?" He hoped not another quick shot to the head, crime scene tape and lots of blood. Katja's ever present firearm made him nervous. It was her security blanket. He was glad that, though Katja always had that darned gun with her, in their apartment she took it off. It looked silly to sit in a bra and panties while wearing a gun belt.

Irwin was afraid of it. When Isaac started walking it could be fatal if the kid picked up that Glock. A woman was killed in a Wal-Mart when her two year old in the shopping cart had found the loaded pistol in her purse.

Katja shook her head. "Here is more safe than the house in Michigan." She glanced at the windows. Since it was a ground floor apartment, the blinds were always drawn at night.

Irwin had to know more. "What kind of local grapevine is there among the Russian community?"

Katja didn't know 'grapevine.' "*Geniznayo*. I don't know."

That was something he needed to find out. He would have to interview Boris if he could work a conversation around to that subject.

At that moment Isaac work up from his nap and starting banging something against the side of his crib. It was Irwin's turn to inspect. When he came back, the conversation had turned to a sitcom on the television. Ivy was hooked on Sex in the City.

. . .

The Saudi students, freed from the religious constraints of their home country and the religious police, were often drunk and noisy. As long as the noise didn't disturb the neighbors on their floor, Irwin didn't mind. He did have to caution them about Portland's strict rules for recycling and composting. He did not like having to sort their stinking garbage. It was one of the unpleasant sides to his job as building manager.

Irwin made a preliminary report to Agent Burke. He called and asked, "What do you know about the local Russian émigré community?"

Burke's knowledge was limited. "There are about five thousand refusenics, Russian Jews who were permitted to leave. There are also a bunch of Evangelical Christians oppressed by the Russian Orthodox Church."

"Kakievich is an engineer on a special work permit, works at Intel."

He could almost see Burke's twisted smile. "A different category. The professionals who are invited here have more status than the peons who simply fled the old Soviet Union. They don't mix."

"Some come for freedom. I guess with Kakievich it's the money. Which is likely to be more political?" He remembered his couple of stinky nights in the drunk tank in Moscow. Those were the poor schmucks whose main interest was not who was president of Russia but where and when could they get that next bottle of rot gut vodka. No wonder the life expectancy of a Russian male had fallen to about fifty-five. They were beyond hope and too sick to bear a grudge against a defector who made it to America.

The professionals might. They had memories. They might have relatives who went to the Gulag for little or no reason. Did Kakievich?

He would have to ask.

On Saturday morning, on the pretext of bringing a supply of biodegradable plastic bags for the compost collection, Irwin knocked at the Kakievich's door. Fortunately Boris was in. "I brought you these," Irwin said.

Boris was puzzled.

Boris Kakievich did not look healthy. He looked soft. His skin was sallow and his eyes didn't seem synchronized, like one looked off in another direction so he kept blinking as if to get them to focus..

"For the compost," Irwin explained, "Only bio-degradables like food scraps go in the compost."

"*Spasebah*. Thanks you."

Irwin hesitated, unsure how to proceed.

Then Boris asked "You have security car I see in the garage?"

"It's a loner. Belongs to the company."

"I am thinking to buy a car. Could you show me?"

Irwin understood. "The commute on the Max must be pretty tedious."

"There are many Mexicans."

So Boris, like other immigrants, was prejudiced again the Others. Maybe it was because he knew English and many of the Spanish-speaking newcomers did not.

Irwin remembered the Russian pejorative for some people: *niet culturni*, no culture. Everyone seemed to look down on someone else. If he chose to, he could look down on Boris who was only a guest worker. That was not his style. Irwin had been a stranger in a strange land and understood.

He remembered being an "other" when riding the bus in Moscow, the looks of envy and derision because he was a foreigner, an American who had access to the commissary, the stores open only to the party elite. If he carried a bag of groceries from the commissary people who had trouble finding meat were curious and envious. What was in his bag? They didn't dare speak to strangers. Russia was a country ruled by fear.

Irwin asked, "What sort of car are you looking for?" He thought of Putinsky's armored SUV. "A Cadillac?"

"A Ford. That is good American car."

"We drive an old police car, a Crown Victoria. I'll show you."

They took the elevator down to the garage.

The security car still had the original rhino bars on the front, but when Irwin opened the door he could see where some of the original police gear had been removed. The bracket for a shotgun was still there, but no fire arm. The was no longer an on board computer monitor.

Boris wanted to see the engine.

Irwin hadn't actually opened the hood. There was no need to. So far he hadn't driven anywhere but to the Safeway grocery a few blocks away. It was a big engine with dual carburetors. How many cylinders did it have? Irwin counted the spark plug wires.

"Very powerful," Boris said, like he knew about cars even though he was a software not a hardware engineer. "This belong to Putinsky?"

"To his security company, yes."

"Does he drive one of these?"

"No," Irwin admitted. "Vladimir has a Cadillac.." He didn't mention that it was armored.

"You call him Vladimir? Not Putinsky?"

"Well, I don't call him Vladi." That would be the Russian diminutive saved for intimates and children.

"How you know him?"

"I met him in Moscow many years ago."

"He was KGB, yes?"

"Yes." Irwin didn't want to go further but Boris knew how to worm information out of someone.

"So how do you, an American, come to know an old KGB?"

"He tried to get me to work for the Russians as a spy."

"How could he do that?"

"He tried to blackmail me with incriminating photographs."

This was an AHA moment for Boris Kakievich. He stood back from the engine of the Security car and looked closely at Irwin Glass. He blinked, focused, and laughed. "I know you. I have seen such pictures."

Irwin was shocked. He had seen the set of photos taken of himself and Katja's mother and handed them over to security at the Embassy. He had never seen them again. "Where did you see them?"

"Six photos. You looked drunk." Boris gave Irwin an admonishing look. "Naughty boy."

Irwin felt embarrassed, upset, surprised, angry all at once. "I was drugged. I don't remember any of it. Do you have those pictures?"

"*Njet*. But they were circulated. There was a secret album of KGB photos, *samizdat*."

Irwin knew that because of censorship some authors had to circulate typed carbon copies of their work among friends, *samizdat*, the underground press. So his own picture had been part of a circulated trove of dirty pictures. Irwin did not have a photo of Katja's mother. The only ones he had seen were Katja's framed in her apartment. "Did the pictures of me show the face of the woman with me?"

Boris winked. "Not her face, just from behind when she was having a nice fuck. And you do not remember?"

"No. I would like to see them myself. Is that possible?"

Boris shook his head. "Not possible." Then he thought of something else. "If Putinsky try to blackmail you, why you work for him now as building manager?"

Irwin closed the hood of the car and locked it with a click of the electronic key. "Those pictures had a result. The result is your neighbor, Katja. She calls herself Katie Glass, but she is Katja Putinsky-Glass. I am her American father."

"Ah," Boris said, like everything was now clear. "Family business. *Horoshaw*. Very good." He laughed. This was a joke worth telling.

As they waited for the elevator Irwin asked, "Besides pictures of me in that samizdat, were there others? Of other men? Other women?"

"Many. Pre-Playboy pornography."

They reached the first floor. Irwin asked, as if it weren't already too late, "Please don't mention those pictures of me in the Russian community."

"Why? Now with internet pornography, your old black and white pictures are of no interest to anyone."

As the door slid shut behind him, Irwin thought, maybe not to anyone, but they sure are to me. He suspected that, bureaucracy and office gossip being what it was, the pictures must have leaked from the KGB offices to satisfy the prurient interest of others. Maybe Putinsky still had the file. He would like to see it.

First he would talk to Ivy.

Ivy was still in her pajamas, there being no need to get dressed. She had Isaac on her lap bouncing him and playing patty-cake. He was laughing, a joyful kid.

"I have news," Irwin said, sitting beside her. "You remember the story I told you about my being photographed and blackmailed by Putinsky back in Moscow?"

She wasn't sure.

"Well, it seems those photographs were circulated along with similar ones, an underground collection of amateur porn."

Ivy was amused. "So you're a porn star? I never guessed." She gave him a look like she was seeing someone else, that he had a secret sideline. "Oooh."

"It's not funny. Neither did I. If Putinsky still has them, would you like to see them? Since they're landmark souvenirs in the story of my downfall in the State Department…"

"If I want to see you naked I can take my own pictures."

Irwin swallowed. "I'm not alone in them. There's Katja's mother."

"You think Katja wants to see her mother having sex with you?"

"I don't know what Katja wants."

"That was when she was conceived, right?"

"So the story goes."

Ivy went back to the game with Isaac. "Seems kind of perverse to me. Sick."

"Knowing that Russians were probably jerking off over pictures of me and Katja's mother makes me sick."

"Then don't bother. Forget it. It was a long time ago."

CHAPTER TWENTY-SIX

Irwin got in the borrowed security car, puzzled over the GPS, decided, since he didn't know Portland's confusing maze of one way streets and freeways, he could at least follow the streetcar tracks over to the east side of the Willamette and find the shopping mall.

He had already been to Putinsky's security offices on the third floor. It was minimum: two rooms, one for the secretary gatekeeper and the back room sanctum sanctorum where shoplifters could be interrogated and detained until the police could arrest them.

The receptionist's knitting project had grown. Now it looked like a scarf in multi colored yarn. She barely nodded to him.

Vladimir Putinsky was pleased to see him, a genuine smile that reached all the way up his face to the top of his bald head. "Irvin! So glad to see you, my friend. How do you like your job?"

"One of the tenants is Boris Kakievich. He recognized me."

"How so?"

"He says the photos you took of me and Katja's mother for that honey pot trap have been circulated as samizdat."

"Oh?" It was feigned surprise. Maybe Vladimir had sold them himself as a sideline.

"Did you have many such pictures? Of other men?"

"Yes. You remember, it was my job."

"Was Katja's mother in all of them?"

"Many." Putinsky fidgeted in his executive office chair. "For the government, I usually hired one of our prostitutes."

So there was a difference. "And when not for the government?"

"If not for the government for my own little side business, blackmail of rich Russians. How do you think I got the money for this?" He gestured at the office. "And for my Mirabella apartment? For the building where you live? It was my nest egg as you call it, for my retirement."

"And Katja's mother was in those so her role was, so to speak, off the books."

Putinsky grinned, showed one stainless steel tooth, the old way Russian dentists did their repair. "Family business."

"Do you still have those pictures? I would like to see them."

Putinsky was hesitant. "I do have them. For insurance. In case I need a new installment from time to time."

"May I borrow them? Ivy wants to see me in my role as a porn star."

Now Putinsky rocked back in his chair and laughed. "Irvin you are turning into a dirty old man."

"I would still like to see them. I don't remember anything of that night except waking up in the street, drunk, in just my under pants."

"For you, Irvin, yes, since you are an old friend." He rotated his chair to face the safe in the corner of the office, turned the dial, opened the door.

Irwin saw stacks of cash inside and other papers. Putinsky's stash, or at least part of it. The rest must be in offshore accounts waiting to be laundered, possibly for another real estate deal, the preferred method of turning clandestine earnings into legitimate assets. There was also an old, well thumbed photo album. He handed it over like a precious artifact.

"Here. But you must return it. I trust you."

Trust me was the appeal used by con artists to invoke trust when there was none.

"You know me," Irwin said, the most non-committal way he could put it.

He took the album, briefly opened it to confirm that it was that kind of photograph, thanked Putinsky and left.

This time he found his way back to the Park Blocks without getting lost.

Once inside the garage, he leafed through the album. The pictures had been taken so the faces of the men were easy to identity, but not necessarily the women. If the woman's hair covered her face as she bent over her supine victim, that didn't matter. What counted was it was clearly sex with someone who would not want the incident known, private enough to pay big money to keep it quiet.

Who were the men? Oligarchs? Congressmen? Ambassadors? Maybe even the president?

Irwin found himself in the bunch. In the years since he first saw the photos he had forgotten. Back then what mattered was the shock and Putinsky's demand that he serve the KGB as an informant. Now it was disappointing. In the photos his eyes looked glazed. He could only see part of Katja's mother's face.

With a sigh he locked the car and took the elevator up to the first floor to show Ivy.

She had put Isaac down in his crib for a nap and was starting to get dressed.

"Here they are," Irwin said like he had bagged an elephant. "Have a look."

She sat down on their bed, just in her panties. "Which ones are you?"

He pointed them out. "And that's Katja's mother."

Ivy was thoughtful. "She looks like she's enjoying herself. On second thought, I think she was taunting the photographer."

Irwin agreed. "She was forced to pose."

"You look pretty good."

"I was in better shape then."

She put down the album and put her hand on his lap. "I bet we could do better than that. Want to have a go?"

"You must be inspired." So was he.

From the nursery they could hear Isaac banging his rattle against the crib like applause.

CHAPTER TWENTY-SEVEN

Katja came by for lunch. She had bought three six-inch Subway sandwiches at the PSU student union to share. While they sat on the high stools at the bar Irwin ruminated over the photos, wondering if he should show them to Katja.

Ivy saved him the trouble. "Irwin has obtained the photos of your conception."

Katja looked up, puzzled. She was in her campus cop uniform again gun and all. "How is that?"

Irwin explained. "Vladimir has a file of such pictures he used for blackmail when he was KGB. Pictures of me and your mother." He gestured toward the album which lay on the counter.

"May I see?"

"Eat first. They might spoil your appetite."

They already had. Katja gulped down the last of her six inch special and took up the album.

Irwin's picture was the first one she saw. She gasped, almost choked. Then she slipped down from the stool, grabbed the album and hurried out.

Ivy was puzzled. "Where's she off to?"

"Probably wants to compare those pictures with the framed photos she has in her place."

"You'd better follow her. This may be traumatic."

"What? Seeing me naked?"

Ivy shook her head. "She's seen that already. It's not about you. It's about her mother."

Irwin got up. "I'd better see how she is."

The elevator didn't come at once. When it did, it brought Mrs. Kakievich. Boris had probably told her about his recollection and the story of Katja Putinsky, AKA Katie Glass. She wanted to chat.

Irwin held the elevator door and escaped quickly. On the fourth floor he knocked at Katja's door. No answer. Worried, he used his own key to let himself in.

He had never before seen Katja cry. She was always cool. Though she could laugh, crying had never been in her repertoire. Now she was, well, broken.

At the Farm he had learned that everyone has a breaking point. That was what an interrogator looked for.

Katja was sobbing over the pictures, her mother's portrait in her lap. She blubbered a stream of unintelligible Russian curses. Irwin gave her his handkerchief to wipe her eyes. When she settled down, she said, between gasps, "Vladimir, that bastard. Son of bitch."

Her hands were wet from her tears. As she fumbled with the glamour portrait of her mother, the backing came loose. Between the photo and the backing was a slip of folded paper, a note. Katja read it quickly, re-read it, and cried some more, grief and anger.

Irwin reached for the note, but she wouldn't let him see it. Finally she handed it over.

The unfamiliar Cyrillic handwriting echoed what Irwin had read when, long ago, as a ten year old, he had found a letter in the attic of their South Bend home. That old letter had set him off on a career in Russian history and language studies. This one was hard for him to make out, for he didn't see much hand written Russian. Unsure of what it said, he handed it back.

Katja had stopped crying. "She says Vladimir ruined her life. She says I must kill him. Let's go now."

"Wait. Take it easy, Katja. Let me see that again."

She handed the note over. There had been changes in Russian script over the years just as the Germans did when they shifted to modern type faces. Irwin had seldom seen any cursive Russian, having always read printed sources. Finally he said, "She wants revenge. She doesn't actually say 'kill him,' does she?"

Katja didn't answer. She was too upset. The note from her mother had a greater affect than the sight of her mother having sex. Irwin wasn't the only partner. It was the forced posing with many men that was so destructive. How could a husband do that to his own wife?

With a flash of understanding Irwin remembered a character in the works of William Faulkner. A character who is himself impotent has to watch other people doing in bed what he himself was incapable of. Was that the case of Vladimir?

Vladimir was such a controlling, manipulative man, so ruthless, a typical sociopath, the kind that makes an effective CEO who is charming on the surface but also has few close friends, only people he can use. He had said, "Irvin, my old friend." Like hell. Irvin my puppet, my tool, my victim.

"We should go see him together, Katja. Confront him with the photos. Get his side of the story."

"Ok."

"Promise?"

She nodded.

"Let's go about five o'clock this afternoon." Then he wondered, did Vladimir have a gun in the office? Was he cold blooded enough to conjure up some back to the wall reason to shoot them both?

Was he worrying too much? Maybe, but that's what he always did: worry.

CHAPTER TWENTY-EIGHT

This time he had no trouble finding the shopping mall. They parked the car on the deck and went to Putinsky's security office. The foreign gatekeeper knew Irwin but not Katja and announced them.

Vladimir feigned pleasure at seeing them but he was nervous, nervous because he read the look on Katja's face and of course saw she was armed as usual. "Ah, Irvin! Katja, my protégé."

Katja was puzzled. "Protégé?"

"You turned out very well. *Horoshaw*. Look at you."

Katja threw the album of incriminating photos down on his desk. "You destroyed my mother's life."

"Bah. Your mother was a whore."

"You forced her to pose for those photographs."

His answer: "A wife does what she is told. She obeys her husband."

"How could you do that to my mother?"

"Will it bother you less to know she was not your mother?"

Irwin caught his breath. He was observing Putinsky closely. Was this another lie? Was this the adroit manipulator of people doing his stuff? The quintessential KGB operative?

Katja was having trouble catching her breath. "What do you mean? Not my mother?"

Putinsky saw his argument was working. He smiled. "Her baby died. I found you in an orphanage and groomed you for your task, raised you to be the perfect assassin, told you Natasha was your mother." He laughed. "How do you like that?"

"But she's my daughter," Irwin protested. "We did the DNA test."

Putinsky looked at Irwin over those wire rimmed glasses. "Faked."

"So this whole thing is a charade? Your nefarious plot?" Irwin didn't have adequate words to curse him, not in Russian or English.

"How do you like that, Irvin, my friend, my puppet?" He turned to Katja. "And he is not your father."

Katja understood. "And you are not my father, either."

"So? I am your puppet master. You follow my orders, as you were trained.." He leaned back in his chair, gloating.

Katja turned to Irwin. "Papa. Wait outside."

As Irwin moved out of the inner office, he heard Putinsky laughing. "He is not your papa. He is mine. I own him."

The door shut.

Irwin did not hear what happened next. He only stood, irresolute, waiting and wondering. It was all too much information to process. That Natasha's baby had died, Katja a substitute her mother seldom saw, all those posed photographs. He could only imagine what went on in her mind, but he did know rebellion was part of it. Beware a woman scorned.

The receptionist who had hardly ever spoken to him asked, "What's happening?"

Katja came out of the inner office, closed the door. Her clothes were rumpled and she smoothed down her jacket.

The Glock was still in its holster as usual. She told the receptionist, "Call 911. Vladimir Putinsky is dead."

"Dead?"

Katja's head tilted back and forth as if choosing between answers. "A stroke. Cerebral hemorrhage I think they call it." Then to Irwin, "Papa, let's go. We have no business here." No remorse. She was her old self again.

She held it together until they got into the car. Then she broke down, sobbing and shaking. Irwin held her in his arms to comfort her.

They sat in the car a long time. When she settled down he dared ask, "Did you kill him? That head lock?"

She could not look him in the eye. "You do not need to know all my secrets, Papa."

Some things you do not want to know.

Back at the Avalon Arms Katja was badly shaken, not by the death of Vladimir Putinsky, which for her might have been an assignment for another hit, but by the revelations about her mother and Irwin. They say in prison there are no guilty parties. The convicted have told themselves so many times they are innocent that they believe it themselves. Vladimir had drummed into Katja the legend that she was Natasha's daughter and that Irwin Glass was her real, American father. It was part of Putinsky's plan. Katja, perhaps, was groomed to be his body guard. Who knew?

Dinner found them sitting together, Ivy, Irwin, Katja and Isaac in his high chair, all but Isaac lost in their own thoughts about their situation. What was real and what was story? That Ivy and Irwin were husband and wife and Isaac their son, that was real. Had Putinsky fabricated his story just to manipulate them all, to make fun of them, to taunt them? If he did, it had backfired.

What had gone wrong?

Katja had changed. For all her spy school training and Putinsky's brain washing, Irwin and Ivy had provided Katja with something missing in her life. It was family. It was family and it was love. Time for a group hug.

They were bound together by that strange history that began in Moscow so many years before. It was not over.

As they might have expected the police arrived, one detective, one uniform. Irwin answered the entry door, went to his concierge's office, saw them on the monitor and let them in.

They were two from the Portland police, a detective in mufti and a uniform. The uniform was a young woman, a choice that facilitated contacts when women wee involved. She was not much older an Katja, who had for the moment gone to the bathroom to avoid a face to face confrontation.

The detective who was about Irwin's age, came into the room and sized up the situation. He saw Katja's gun belt hanging from the back of her bar stool and was instantly on his guard. "We're looking for Irwin Glass."

"That's me." Irwin knew full well what they wanted to know but pretended to be innocent, something he wasn't very good at. "What's up?"

"You were at the security office of Vladimir Putinsky."

"That's right."

":When the 911 call came in saying he was dead."

"Yes."

"Why didn't you wait for the ambulance?"

"He was dead. There was no point." Like what's the big deal? He's only another dead person.

The detective was taking notes on a well-worn pocket notebook. "What do you know about Vladimir Putinsky?"

Irwin didn't want to go into the whole story, the first Moscow confrontation, the interrogation at the Farm, all that history. "I don't think I can tell you about that. I've been working on the case with the FBI. We don't discuss investigations in progress."

This was an excuse the detective hadn't heard before.

Ivy didn't wait for an invitation. "Irwin was working on a terrorism case in Michigan. When that was over, they brought us to Portland to keep an eye on Putinsky." She didn't mention Katja.

As if on cue, Katja returned from the bathroom, saw the police and moved quietly to her bar stool, put on her gun belt.

The uniform stiffened.

"Careful," Irwin cautioned. "This is Katja, my daughter. She's with campus security. Don't draw your weapon on her." He knew she could draw and fire unerringly if threatened. He didn't want another shooting, all that blood, all those complications, crime scene tape, best to keep things calm.

"She have a permit for that?"

"Yes. But she's upset. It's been a harrowing day, difficult for all of us. Vladimir Putinsky was sort of family. His death is a shock."

"Sorry for your loss." It was that standard condolence statement, conventional and meaningless, not that Irwin, Ivy and Katja felt any loss at all. They were glad he was dead..

Irwin explained, "If you want to know more about Vladimir Putinsky, I suggest you call Agent Burke of the local FBI office. He has the files."

The detective wrote down the agent's name. He turned to Katja. "And you are?"

"Katie Glass," Katja said, falling back on her Portland pseudonym.

"The receptionist at the security office said you found the body."

"Vladimir was dead."

The detective was hoping for more. "Dead?"

"Dead like a dog," said with no more emotion than if Putinsky had been a rat run over on the highway. She was back to her cold killer self.

"What was your relationship with Vladimir Putinsky?"

Katja smiled as if at a private joke. "He was my father."

The detective took a deep breath while he absorbed that one. "I thought Irwin Glass is your father."

Irwin intervened. "It's complicated. We are, well, an unusual family. I think you should talk first to Agent Burke."

The police left. Irwin followed them out, made sure the front door to the Avalon Arms was locked. When he came back Katja was laughing. She gave him a hug and a kiss on the mouth. Yes, they were an unusual family. No doubt about that.

CHAPTER TWENTY-NINE

The next morning Irwin drove down to the FBI office and parked the security car in a handicapped spot, gambling that he would not get a ticket.

Agent Burke was in. Irwin started by saying, "You were right. Katja was a sleeper agent. What Putinsky didn't know was the trigger to activate her came from her mother."

"How's that?"

"A note. It said that Putinsky ruined her mother's life and Katja should take revenge."

"Do you have the note?"

Irwin shook his head. "Sorry." It might be evidence he did not want to possess.

Agent Burke was eager to hear the story.. "I heard that Putinsky is dead, had a stroke in his office."

"That's the story," Irwin said, knowing Burke was smart enough to know there was more.

"Did she kill him?"

"Who?"

"Katja, of course, your fake daughter."

Irwin put on a shrug, like how do I know? "I didn't see anything."

"Did she confess?"

"What? Let's just say Vladimir Putinsky is dead and let that be the end of it."

"So what did you come to see me for?"

"Those files? The ones you showed me?"

Burke still had his morning coffee and sipped it, noted it was cold, and set the cup asides. "Sure. What about it?"

"It has Katja's Russian birth certificate in it."

Burke found the file and leafed through it, found the document. "Here it is." He handed it to Irwin. "In Russian, of course."

"I read Russian." Irwin carefully examined the copy and smiled. "Putinsky did his homework well. This birth certificate says Katja is his daughter. Of course, being KGB he could fabricate any document."

Burke admitted, "I don't get it."

"It means Katja is Putinsky's heir. She inherits everything, the Mirabella flat, the Avalon Arms, Putinsky's businesses." He remembered the cash he saw in the safe. "Everything." He didn't mention whatever secret offshore accounts Putinsky used to stash his loot. "Her name is already on some joint accounts. She's rich.

Agent Burke suddenly had a new respect for Irwin Glass. "If she killed him, she can't inherit."

"No proof. I think the autopsy will show a cerebral hemorrhage."

Burke was appalled. "She's killed people."

"Never charged."

"And you live with that woman?" Like, do you sleep with cobras?

"She's family. She needs us. We're her anchor. Without us…" He knew what Katja was capable of.

Burke had a suspicion. "You all sleep in the same bed?"

"Sometimes."

Burke scratched his head. "My God."

Irwin got ready to leave. He took a copy of the Russian birth certificate with him. "Oh, hang onto those files. There may be items we need later."

Burke shook his head in disbelief. "You know, Glass, you're not a simpleton, after all."

"Never said I was."

He did not get a parking ticket and did not think he would have to park there again anyway. He was through with the FBI. There was nobody left to inform on.

Back at the apartment he showed Katja the Russian birth certificate. He explained, "Katja, I don't know if what Vladimir said about your origins is true or not, but here is a birth certificate that says you are his daughter."

"So?"

"It means that you are his sole heir. You own everything. How about that for your mother's revenge?"

"But if she was not really my mother?"

Ivy had the answer to that. "It doesn't matter. She loved you."

You have to have faith in your own legend.

That night, after Isaac was tucked away in his crib Ivy and Irwin snuggled down for some pillow talk. Ivy said, "You know, honey, if Katja really isn't your real daughter I have a suggestion."

"What's that?"

"Why don't we all get together and make Isaac a baby sister?"

"You mean, like a team effort?"

He thought about it. He remembered that wild threesome romp. Sounded pretty good. "What do you think Katja would say about it?" Of course, there was no guarantee any baby they made with Katja would be a girl.

Ivy kissed him. "You and I both know it's not good to be an only child. I think she'd love the idea. Irwin, it's family." Family was everything.

"What about incest?"

"Not if she's not your real daughter."

181

Irwin was a Midwesterner and had misgivings. South Bend, Indiana was conventional and reserved, even dull, except at the Notre Dame football games. "What about adultery?"

Ivy had an answer for that, too. "Not if you have permission." She smiled. Isaac was going to love having a baby sister.

Before he fell asleep, Irwin had another thought. Nudging Ivy he said, "You know, what you do changes your brain. You may not have noticed, but since you had Isaac you're a different person. You've become a mother."

"I have?"

"Yes, and if Katja becomes a mother I think that will change her, too, from being a trained killer to being a nurturer." He thought of Katja as a mother, nursing a baby. Being a mother was a different life. Since they had Isaac Irwin and Ivy's relationship had changed, too. Now they were parents. It was a good thing. Maybe it would be a good thing if Katja was carrying a baby instead of a Glock. It was something to hope for.

"What if Katja doesn't agree?"

Ivy seemed to know the answers to everything. "She will.

About Harley L. Sachs:

Though born in Chicago and raised in Indiana, Harley L. Sachs considers himself an international, having lived in Germany, Sweden, Scotland, and Denmark. He earned a degree in English at Indiana University, then served in the US Army in Germany. After getting his Master's degree at I.U. he returned to Europe and worked under cover for several years. He met and married Ulla in Stockholm, Sweden and they spent a year's honeymoon in a Scottish castle. Returning to the USA, Sachs taught English briefly at Southern Illinois University then moved to Michigan Technological University in the Upper Peninsula where he and his wife raised three daughters. He took early retirement and now lives in Portland, Oregon.

Harley L. Sachs

Here's a list of books by Harley L. Sachs:

MYSTERY NOVELS

The Mystery Club Series

THE MYSTERY CLUB SOLVES A MURDER
First and most popular of the Mystery Club series. Mary Higgins finds the body of Dora Reed on the roof of the Plaza retirement building, notifies the police, then tells the Mystery Club. They assume several suspects: the manager of the Plaza, Dora's son Donald, or a Plaza employee. Dora's husband, Ed Sutherland, is in Hawaii on board the yacht Miss Chief with an all girl crew. Carrying on their own investigation, the Mystery Club finally suspects Sutherland, though he seems to have a perfect alibi. If they can prove it to their satisfaction, will a court ever convict him-- if he can be found somewhere in the Pacific?

THE MYSTERY CLUB AND THE DEAD DOCTOR
Second in the Mystery Club series. The Mystery Club consists of five elderly women who live at the Rose Plaza and discuss mysteries written by women. The Mystery Club ladies have no idea of the consequences when Viola Cartwright, their blind member, asks them to go over her Medicare bills. That leads to suspicion about the identity of her personal assistant, Dorothy Anderson, who turns out to be using a stolen identity. Viola's doctor runs a phony clinic owned by a member of the Russian Mafia. Soon the investigation of Medicare bills leads to murder and tragedy, stopped only by the courage of Mary Higgins.

THE MYSTERY CLUB AND THE HIDDEN WITNESS
Third in the Mystery Club series. The ladies of the Mystery Club discover one of the residents is a crook under WITSEC, the witness protection program. He apparently keeps dipping into the employee gift fund. The Mystery Club bands together to track down the missing money, but what they discover is danger.

THE MYSTERY CLUB AND THE SERIAL WIDOW
Fourth in the Mystery Club series. Caroline Kostinsky, new resident at the Rose Plaza, is a widow four times over and she's looking for a fifth husband in retired General Hardcastle, but when drunk she says she killed all of her husbands. Except for her confession, there's no evidence. Now what?

DELIVER ME FROM EVIL
Responding to a posted invitation for new members for the Mystery Club, Judge Ira Kahane and Ursula Besette show up. Ursula, at a turning point in her life as a new Rose Plaza resident, is interested in Wicca and Kabala. Roberta Nelson believes one should not suffer a witch to live. Judge Kahane tries to lead Ursula on the right path, but there is conflict and tragedy coming.

WHITE SLAVE
Sequel to *The Mystery Club Solves a Murder.* The appearance of Ed Sutherland's gold bracelet in a Portland pawn shop revives retired detective Casey's interest in the cold case. He doesn't know that Sutherland has been picked up and is a slave on a Korean fishing boat. Sutherland, penniless, .without clothes or identification, is stranded in New Zealand. Can he find his way back to Portland and be somehow redeemed or face a death sentence for first degree murder?

The Irwin Glass Series

BETRAYAL
Prequel to *Retribution.* Irwin Glass, BA in Russian, MA in International Relations, has a promising career in the Foreign Service in Moscow until he is snared in a classic "honey pot" seduction. He's young and naïve, honest, always wants to do the right thing, but at every turn he is betrayed. The incident in Moscow destroys his career. He is accused of being a paid Soviet agent and is pursued by the consequences of his encounter with the KGB twenty years later. Some enemies never let go

RETRIBUTION
Sequel to *Betrayal.* Newly married to Ivy Hartshorn, Irwin Glass gets a dunning letter from the IRS for taxes on interest at the Washington, DC account he didn't think he had. It's a joint account with his missing birth daughter and the balance is huge. Assuming it's money Katya's KGB father of record, Vladimir Putinsky (now Putin) deposited for her living expenses, Irwin moves it to force her to contact him. But Ivy warns him that he is laundering money and the people it belongs to will come after him. Irwin's complicated life is catching up with him, but this time he will find retribution.

BURNT OUT
Irwin Glass is approached by FBI Agent Wilkins who asks for Irwin's lists of foreign students. Not satisfied he wants more and is looking for potential terrorists among the Moslem students. Gradually Irwin is sucked

into the role of FBI informant on the Michigan Institute of Technology's Muslim Students' Association and the results are tragic.

THE IRWIN GLASS TRILOGY

All three Irwin Glass books in one package deal. The Irwin Glass Trilogy combines all three of the Irwin Glass Mysteries: "Betrayal," "Retribution," and "Burnt Out," following the chaotic career of Irwin Glass who began, in "Betrayal," as a state department clerk in Moscow only to be caught in a classic honey pot seduction. Betrayed at every turn, he was sent back to the United States in disgrace to try to start a new life. No such luck. His teaching career is upturned by the revelation that the Moscow seduction had a consequence in the form of a beautiful student Katya who claims to be his daughter. In "Retribution," Irwin's KGB nemesis is in the United States seeking political asylum, but in fact is fleeing the Russian Mafia with Irwin as quarry. After "Retribution," Irwin thinks he is home free of all that intrigue, but the local FBI agent has a hold on him and wants information about potential terrorists among Irwin's students at Michigan Institute of Technology. There are risks to being a reluctant FBI informant, and Irwin's reports may be misconstrued with tragic results. What Irwin and his wife really want is a normal life, but his mysterious Russian birth daughter Katya remains an enigma. Is she or isn't she?

KATJA

"Katja" is the sequel to the Irwin Glass trilogy, "Betrayal," "Retribution," and "Burnt Out." From the time Katja turned up outside the office of Irwin Glass, instructor at Michigan Institute of Technology, claiming she is his daughter, she was an enigma. She is beautiful, sexy, and alluring but she is also a trained cold-blooded killer who carries a Glock 9 millimeter pistol. As his alleged daughter, she becomes a dangerous member of Irwin's household. The FBI claim she is a sleeper agent, suggesting there is a trigger to activate her for her ultimate mission, but what is it? When Irwin, Ivy and baby Isaac join Katja in Portland, Oregon, we find out, but how do you cure a trained assassin of homicidal tendencies?

Other Mysteries

MURDER BY MAIL (Scratch--Out!)

German exchange student Klaus Hitz is more interested in making money than in asking questions about his work assignment. He doesn't know that the industrialist father of his punk girl friend is using him in a terrorist conspiracy to kill everyone in the United States with a mass mailing of a scratch and sniff virus. The plot begins to unravel when a Polish nurse brings blood samples from Libya and alerts a CIA agent. While the CIA and FBI track down the terrorists, Klaus Hitz gradually figures it out.   How can he avoid being murdered or imprisoned for being naive?

MURDER IN THE KEWEENAW
CIA agent recovering from Post traumatic Stress after failed missions in Finland and a divorce is fishing in Lake Superior when he snags a corpse. He thinks he has seen the girl before and his attempt to identify her leads him to a ring of deadly pornographers. It almost costs him his own life.

CONSPIRACY!
Technical writer Tom Godot can't believe his luck when CONSPIRACY!, the book he has co-written with the elusive Harold Stevenson, is a hit. The book details a plot to hijack communication satellites.   As Tom crosses the country on his book tour, he is disturbed by people interested in early drafts and dogged by an NSA agent.   Communicating by fax with his editor and by encrypted e-mail with the mysterious Stevenson, Tom reaches out in his loneliness to his California girl friend Sylvia Hanson who turns out to be a pivotal figure.   There is another conspiracy, and Tom is part of it

THE GOLD CHROMOSOME
When Adam Rottman's childless Aunt Sadie Gold died, the eight cousins learned her estate was in an irrevocable trust, the proceeds going to Adam's sister Sarah while she lives.   After Sarah's death, the money would go to the last surviving cousin.   It's a fatal tontine Adam's lawyer brother Harold set up.   Would the cousins kill each other for one million dollars? Sarah's car is found in the river, but not Sarah.   That begins a series of mysterious deaths.   Coincidence? Or Murder? Who will be next? Adam and his psychologist wife Deborah must stop the chain before he, too, is eliminated.

BEN ZAKKAI'S COFFIN
Born of a Jewish father and a Catholic mother, Herman Bachrach insists he has no religion, but he is drawn by circumstance into a holocaust vendetta over gold stolen by a Swiss bank from Jewish depositors. Seduced by a woman who calls herself Diana, no last name, Herman is suspected by detective Sheehan to be her murderer.   Someone else wants him dead.   His Jewish boss provides him with a lawyer, but sends him to Switzerland to finish the job "Diana" started.   It's an assignment he can't refuse.   The result is an epiphany of identity that changes Herman's life forever.

THE LOLLIPOP MURDER
A warning for wannabe novelists! What happens when a stable of neurotic novelists who live in their pseudonyms and are bound by iron clad contracts are invited aboard their miserly Florida publisher's yacht for the Miami Book Fair only to find that they have no hope of ever earning a dime of royalties for their books? All this as Hurricane Gerta threatens to sink the yacht at the dock. It's grounds for murder

DEAD MEN DON'T BLEED
Being transgender is tough. A grisly murder of a Vietnam vet on the top floor of the Rose Plaza retirement building is a challenge for Detective Carol, previously Caryl. As a ransgender person she is not accepted by the Portland police, nor is a vice cop convert to Islam. The pair team up to solve the crime and prove they have what it takes to be respected on the force..

NOVELS

SAM IN LOVE
A coming of age romance for mature young adults. U.S. Army life in Europe in the 1950's was an equivalent of the Grand Tour of the eighteenth century when young men traveled and sowed wild oats. Marty, roommate of Sam Logan, a PFC draftee serving in the US Army in Munich, Germany, says all Sam needs is to get laid. Sam is not a virgin, but has a Midwestern ethic and believes in love. He doesn't know quite what that is. No Casanova, Sam, through a series of tentative encounters, thinks he's found the love of his life.

STOPRAPE.COM
Kerstin Mikkola, a young TV reporter at KDUP in Marquette, Michigan has hopes of a better network job. Her interview with a marine victim or rape might be just the ticket. Her interview about the web site StopRape.com goes viral on U-tube and Kerstin finds herself in the thick of consequences she did not anticipate.

THE ACCIDENTAL COURIER
A romance, road trip, and mystery all in one. Charles Kosko, retired orchard owner from Oregon, decides to take a bus trip in Europe and finds himself involved in a whistle-blower's scheme to discredit an American cell phone company that uses rare earths mined by slaves in the Congo. Unable to speak any foreign language, and without his US passport, he is picked up by a beautiful Israeli woman who says she is his

driver. But is he really her prisoner? They are pursued by an African mining engineer, who hopes to intercept the delivery of stolen rare earths,

The Harvey Goldstein Series:

THE SEVENTH PARADIGM: HARVEY GOLDSTEIN IS WATCHING YOU.
Harvey Goldstein does the grocery coupons for the Krieger grocery chain and wants to know everything about everybody.. On a visit to Hamburg with a distant Uncle Julius, ex stasi secret policeman, Harvey is warned about the Seventh Paradigm. It all has to do with metadata. By the time he finds out what it is, it may be too late.

HARVEY GOLDSTEINN AND THE METADATA CURSE
Harvey has a "gift" of a million stolen bitcoins from the mysterious "Angel," but he is afraid the owners will want it returned or at least revenge. But who gave it to him? And where did it come from? He might be Metadata Man, but he is no super hero? He and Ursula try to track down the elusive "Angel"

HARVEY GOLDSTEIN INTERNET COP
The mysterious "Angel" turns out to be Gulli. Harvey tracks her down and gives her a proposition she cannot refuse. Just as technology over-ran Harvey's job at Krieger, a new phone app threatens to undo all his advantages as Metadata Man.

All three Harvey Goldstein mysteries are bundled into a single trilogy volume.

SCI-FI AND FANTASY

NEVER TRUST A TALKING HORSE
The narrator of this dystopian novel escapes preventive detention into a world he discovers has gone mad. Hungry, he is told he can eat for free at Lachumba's supper club, only to discover that he might be the main dish. He rescues Iris I. Iris from the ovens and in a series of episodes explores the insane world in search of a livelihood. He gradually realizes why he was incarcerated in the first place, but by then it is too late. His and Iris's roles have been reversed. Arrested, they are given a sadistic sentence which is their final challenge.

THE SEARCH FOR JESSE BRAM

Jesse Bram, the young hero of this metaphysical science fiction adventure, is unaware of his Jewish roots. An Eldre of mixed breed, he is marooned on the post apocalyptic shunned planet URth where technology and books have been destroyed.   The URthlings variously view Jesse as a bringer of cargo for the half-breed prefect Hrod, as the reborn Savior by crypto-Christians, and as a link to the past by a remnant of Jews.   The Galactic Federation suspects him of treason and he is pursued by an enigmatic Trinian policeman.   If Jesse survives, will he be convicted? If acquitted, what next?

SHORT STORIES

THREADS OF THE COVENANT: THE JEWS OF RED JACKET
A collection of twenty-one short stories about Jewish life in small town America centering about two main characters, David Katz, the only Jewish boy in Red Jacket, and Richard Goldman, the only Jewish professor at Copper country Community College. Each story depicts another aspect of what it means to be a Jew in a small town as each character comes to realize his own identity.

MISPLACED PERSONS
Though set in different locales what these stories have in common is a central character who is out of his element, in the wrong place, coming to grips with cultural, generational, or physical displacement.   In PROBLEM FOR THE TEACHER an expatriate fumbles for a living; in LIMBO an ex-G.I. is adrift in Copenhagen; in TRIUMPH OF THE WILL a nervous wreck seeks recuperation; in MISCALCULATION a would be tax evader succumbs to his own fears; in THE LIE a drunk gets himself into difficulties, and in THE GIRLS OF FREDERIKSHAVN an old man is trapped by girls looking for action.

YOOPER TALES AND OTHER FUNNY STUFF
Extracted from the massive volume of Sachs's published Essays and Columns: 1992-2011, this collection of stories related to Michigan's Upper Peninsula, known as the UP, home of Yoopers, reveals the truth about snow fleas, ice worms, the humungous fungus (world's largest living thing) and the rigors of winters in the remote north woods. You can also learn how to catch and cook the Mosquito Giganticus and why visitors won't come. Sachs has several awards for his humor.

AHOY! QUARTERDECK!
Originally published as IRMA QUARTERDECK REPORTS but re-released with new illustrations and, in the paperback edition, with sea shanties, this funny book is a series of boating anecdotes about Irma and

her bumbling husband Ralph ("I can't believe I lost the anchor") Quarterdeck in their many boating adventures and mishaps. One reviewer says the book is as informative as Chapman's famous manual, but more fun. Readers will find plenty of laughs in this book and at the same time learn a great deal of boating fundamentals.

ANNA-LENA'S TROLL AND OHER STORIES
Each of the three Sachs daughters has a story in this children's book. "Anna-Lena's Troll" explores the nature of trolls, which represent the dark side of human behavior as Anna-Lena's nasty letter to Santa is rewarded by the gift of a nasty troll. "The Return of Baby Suzy" is the true story of Cynthia's worn out doll and its resurrection. "The Stars for Christmas" is the remarkable surprise Belinda got along with her new eye glasses. Other family stories are Christmas related.

NON-FICTION

THE MISADVENTURES OF CPL. SACHS
Adrift through college at Indiana University, author Sachs was drafted at the end of the Korean War. Physically unfit for combat, he was sent to Queer Company for basic training, then by a fluke was shipped out to Germany instead of Korea. Thus began his own version of the traditional Grand Tour.

FREELANCE NONFICTION ARTICLES
This third edition of a monograph on freelance writing first published by the Society for Technical Communication is newly updated. This little manual provides tips for interviewing, article structure, article preparation and submission, photography, and business practice.

CHILLY-CHILLY-BANG—HOW WE FREELANCED THROUGH EUROPE'S COLDEST WINTER IN A VW WITH A KID
Companion piece to *Freelance Nonfiction Articles*. The former is a how to book. This is a "how we did it" memoir. The author knew nothing about Volkswagens when they set off, but as they worked from VW dealer to dealer getting the old Combi fixed, he learned! It's as much a book for VW enthusiasts as it is for writers.

Both FREELANCE NONFICTION ARTICLES and *Chilly-Chilly-BANG! How we Freelanced Through Europe's Coldest Winter in a VW with a Kid* are combined in a double volume, *The Writing Life*.

THE 1957 SACHS ARCTIC EXPEDITION
After military service in Germany the author took the GI Bill to Sweden. With no income in the summer, and not even sure there was a road to the far north, he set off hitchhiking to North Cape, the northernmost point in Europe in search of the midnight sun. Illustrated.

FROM TENT TO CASTLE: MEMOIR OF A YEAR LONG HONEYMOON
Setting off from Stockholm, Sweden on rebuilt one speed bicycles, Harley and Ulla embarked on an open-ended honeymoon with no fixed destination and equipped with a tent, a thin double sleeping bag, a tiny gasoline stove, and $3000. After arriving in Britain, Ulla discovered she was pregnant. Tired of unrelenting rain, they advertised for a cheap place to spend the winter. They were offered the gatehouse to Borthwick Castle outside Edinburgh, Scotland for $25 a month by British author Theo Lang.

"IS"
As Bill Clinton said, "It all depends on what the meaning of "is" is."
A problem we all have is distinguishing between what is real and what is not. This is in fact an age-old question. This volume switches between classical instances of the problem to the author and his psychiatrist and his wife. What is real? That all depends on the meaning of "real."

QUEER COMPANY
Not a gay novel, this is a fictionalized memoir of an experimental basic training unit at the end of the Korean War. All the draftees were physically unfit for combat but the army didn't want to discharge them. Instead they got modified training in a company unfortunately designated Q. In the Army phonetic alphabet Q is Queen, but Q company was called queer. A copy is in the US Army historical archives.

www.ingramcontent.com/pod-product-compliance
Lightning Source LLC
Chambersburg PA
CBHW020959180626
46814CB00003B/1175